Die Laughing

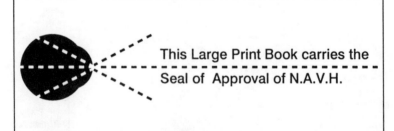

Die Laughing

RICHARD LOCKRIDGE

Thorndike Press • Thorndike, Maine

Library of Congress Cataloging in Publication Data:

Lockridge, Richard, 1898-
    Die laughing / by Richard Lockridge.
        p. cm.
    ISBN 1-56054-240-3 (alk. paper : lg. print)
    1. Large type books. I. Title.
[PS3523.O245D54   1992]   91-40154
813'.52—dc20   CIP

Thorndike Press Large Print edition published in 1992
by arrangement with HarperCollins Publishers, Inc.

Large Print edition available in the British Commonwealth
by arrangement with Curtis Brown, Ltd.

Cover design by Carol Pringle.

The tree indicium is a trademark of Thorndike Press.

This book is printed on acid-free, high opacity paper.

For Hildy

I

This is what Patrolman Williams (J. K.) saw at five minutes after five on the afternoon of Sunday, the eighth of June, and, in due course and the official language prescribed, reported to precinct:

He was walking — officially, he was proceeding — east on Point Street, which has that name for only a block in its meandering course through the West Village. It was a warm day without being a hot one, and the wind from the west pushed him gently along his beat. He was not expecting anything; on that part of his beat he seldom expected anything which would concern a policeman and almost always he was right. There the houses are old and, with few exceptions, of uniform height, which is four stories. Many of the houses there are occupied by single families, although some have been remodeled to provide floor-through apartments.

It is almost sedate in the block which is Point Street. There are, commonly, no hippies nearer than Eighth Street. The street was almost deserted as Patrolman Williams walked the block. There were not even many cars parked at the curbs. The cars of the residents of Point Street were in Westchester County and in Fairfield County and in New Jersey.

As he entered the Point Street block, Patrolman Williams had been hailed anxiously by a couple in a green Pontiac with Connecticut plates. They were expected for cocktails by a friend who lived in Patchin Place and they had, they were sure they had, gone precisely as he had told them. So where — where on earth? — was something called Patchin Place?

They were, Patrolman Williams told them, headed directly, or as directly as was possible, away from it. The best way to get there —

He told them and they listened. Right at the second intersection, and a block on and then right again. Then diagonally to the left, because the street they would be on turned one-way against them. At the intersection of West Fourth and West Tenth Streets they —

Patrolman Williams wished them luck and did not voice his great doubt that they would have it. Greenwich Village, West or East, is not a simple place for aliens. It is not entirely coherent even for those who live in it.

Williams walked on to the east. He was four

doors from Mrs. Singleton's house, which was twice as wide as any other house in the block, when the front door of the wide house opened violently and a tall man came out of the house in a leap. He jumped the three white steps which led from door to sidewalk and began to run east. He ran like a very young and active man. He wore tight dungarees and a white skivvy shirt.

Patrolman Williams didn't like any part of it. He reached for his gun, although he wasn't going to shoot anybody for running, and yelled, "Hey, you!" He went into a trot after the running man. There was no point in trying to match the runner's speed. Years younger than I am, Williams thought. A kid, really. "Hey, you!"

And the kid turned and began to run back toward Williams, who stopped and waited.

It was a kid, all right. Six feet or near it; blond hair and a wide forehead and blue eyes. A nice-looking kid. A kid who had, from the look of his dungarees, been kneeling in soft earth. Earth stains, pretty surely. But the stain on the white skivvy shirt wasn't the brown of earth.

"All right, son," Williams said, "what's the great hurry?"

"She's dead," the boy said. "I found her and she's dead. *Dead*, I tell you. Somebody

9

shot her or stabbed her."

The boy's voice went high, shrill. It shook. He shouted, although he was very close to the patrolman. Pretty close to hysteria, Williams thought.

"All right," Williams said. "Take it easy, son. Who's dead?"

"Mrs. Singleton," the boy said. "She lives there." He pointed.

Williams knew where Jennifer Singleton lived. Everybody knew who she was and where she lived and that the house she lived in had been designated a "landmark." And that it was appropriate that Jennifer Singleton should live in such a house.

"All right, son," Patrolman Williams said. "Let's go have a look. Maybe Mrs. Singleton just cut herself, accidental like."

He didn't think so. The stain on the boy's skivvy shirt was pretty certainly blood. He took the boy by a tanned, strong arm and they went back into the landmark mansion the boy had fled from until a policeman yelled at him.

II

It had been a bright day in early June, and after they had, together, walked the little Scotty bitch named Cleo and peeked at the New York *Times,* they had gone under the East River to Manhattan and Central Park. They had walked there in the sun — walked between benches on which old men dozed in the sun and nursemaids chattered contentedly, with occasional glances at baby carriages. They had avoided being knocked over by strenuous people on bicycles. It had been entirely pleasant, and they had gone to the zoo. A lioness was in her outside cage, lying stretched out in the sun.

They had lunched at the cafeteria and because they were late had found a table on the terrace. Afterward they had ridden downtown on a Fifth Avenue bus and walked through Washington Square and to the Seventh Avenue subway. They had gone back under the river to Brooklyn. They had had dinner at a German restaurant near their apartment.

Cleo had been glad to see them when they went into the apartment. She was firm, however, about being taken for another walk, and Nathan Shapiro took her. She was more cooperative than she often was. Altogether it was a most pleasant Sunday, and Nathan was back in time to turn on the radio for the Sunday evening symphony.

Back in the apartment, Shapiro could take his gun off and put it on the closet shelf where it lived when it did not live on Nathan Shapiro, lieutenant, New York Police Department. When he was not in the apartment it always lived on him, even when, on an off-duty Sunday, he strolled with Rose in Central Park and looked at lionesses lying stretched out in the sunshine.

Rose brought in a bottle of wine and a small glass on a tray. She brought in a gin and tonic for herself. She put the tray down on a table and looked pointedly at the wine bottle and shook her head at it.

"It's a summer day," Rose Shapiro said. "A day for a cold drink. I could put it in a tall glass on ice and add a little soda and —"

She stopped because Nathan was, gently, shaking his head at her. He smiled as he shook his head and the smile changed his long face. The sadness native to it was, if only momentarily, dissipated by the smile, although the

12

smile was one of rejection. The smile reached even to his sad dark eyes.

"It's sweet," Rose said. "It's sticky. The only thing to be said for it is that it's kosher."

"Well," Nathan said, "I am the son of a rabbi, darling."

"Not to that extent," Rose said, and sat down, holding her own glass. "I've known you to —"

She stopped because the radio, which had been speaking with marked enthusiasm about a brand of yoghurt, said, "And now the news. The police are questioning an eighteen-year-old high-school senior named Roy Baker in connection with the fatal stabbing today of Jennifer Singleton, Broadway star for many years. According to the police, it was young Baker who found her body in the second-floor bedroom suite of her home on Point Street, in Greenwich Village. According to the police, the youth was picked up as he was leaving Miss Singleton's house, which is listed as a landmark. In Vietnam, twenty-four marines were killed and seventy-five wounded when they were ambushed during mopping-up operations in the western highlands area. South Vietnamese troops involved in what is officially described as a joint operation are reported to have suffered no casualties. Cairo charged today that —"

Cairo's charge ended in a click. Rose Shapiro moves quickly when she feels a need for quickness. The big radio phonograph wheezed slightly and was silent.

"So?" Nathan Shapiro said. "Egypt is usually charging something."

"Nathan," Rose said. "Didn't you listen?"

"Yes," Nathan Shapiro said. "Jennifer Singleton has been killed. I'm sorry. She was a fine actress. Perhaps even a great actress. I'm sorry when anyone is killed, darling."

She nodded quickly, but the nod dismissed. It wasn't, Nathan Shapiro realized, because of shock at hearing of Jennifer Singleton's death that she had clicked off the radio.

"The boy," she said. "They named the boy. Which means — what does it mean?"

"At a guess," Shapiro said, "because they're pretty sure he's the one they want, Rose."

"If they are they're wrong," Rose Shapiro said. "Wrong as they can be. I know the boy, Nate. He's a fine boy. I *know* him, Nate."

Nathan Shapiro shook his memory briefly and a name sifted out — Roy Baker. He repeated it aloud. He said, "It isn't an uncommon name, Rose. Probably there are dozens of Roy Bakers going to high schools in the five boroughs. No reason to think this is your Roy Baker."

"He's a member of the student council,"

14

Rose said, still standing by the radio phonograph. "He's been in my office several times. With other members, usually. He's a fine boy, Nathan. What did you say?"

"That there are probably a good many boys named Roy Baker going to New York high schools," Nathan Shapiro said. He spoke gently. Rose is seldom excited. She was then. It is a good thing to be gentle with the excited, especially when they are also the loved.

"Nathan," Rose said, "I *know* the boy. And I know about him. He wants to go to college and he ought to go to college. His mother is dead and he lives with his father some place in the Village. On Morton Street, I think it is. And his father is a grocery clerk or something like that and there isn't much money. He works after school and on Sundays, I think, and —"

She broke off and went back to her chair and drank from her tall glass, apparently without knowing that she did so.

She identifies herself too much, Nathan Shapiro thought — too much with the boys and girls who go to the schools she teaches in. Or, as now — as since the autumn before — helps direct. The autumn before Rose Shapiro, a high-school teacher in Brooklyn for some years — a teacher of English — had been made an assistant principal and been transferred to a school which needed one. The school happened to be in Greenwich Village, but Greenwich Village in Manhattan is not too many subway stops from Brooklyn.

She identifies with the kids, Nathan thought. And, because she is a sensitive and perceptive person, she gets to know a good deal about them. And I suspect she is usually right about them. The symphony, Shapiro decided, would have to wait its turn.

He went to the telephone at the other end of the living room and dialed and heard, "Homicide South, Detective Cook."

"Evening, Tony," Shapiro said and gave his own name. He did not preface it with the word "Lieutenant," partly because he did not need to with Anthony Cook, detective, first grade, and largely because Nathan Shapiro regards his rather recent promotion as an outstanding, and incomprehensible, mistake on the part of the Police Department of the City of New York. When possible, he avoids referring to this colossal error in judgment.

"About this Jennifer Singleton killing," Shapiro said. "Want to give me a rundown, Tony?"

"Put you on to Lieutenant Conley?"

"No need to bother him," Shapiro said. "Just a once-over will do, Tony. This kid who's been picked up. Happen he goes to Clayton High?"

"Did," Anthony Cook said. "I'd put it that way, Lieutenant. On account of it looks like they've got him cold. Couple of our boys are checking it out, but the way it looks precinct's got him cold. Seems —"

Shapiro listened for several minutes. He asked one or two questions. One of them was, "Any idea what the kid looks like, Tony?"

"White boy," Anthony Cook told him. "Blond hair and blue eyes. Nice-looking kid, for what good that's going to do him. Unless they get women on the jury."

"Charged?"

"Not yet, far's I know. Maybe the material-witness gimmick. If you're specially interested, Lieutenant, I'll get what else I can and call you back. You home now?"

"Yes," Shapiro said. "I'm not all that interested, Tony. Happened to hear about it on the radio and got curious. Inquisitive, like the book says to be."

"The book" is *Rules and Regulations and Manual of Procedure*, Police Department, City of New York. It says: "A good detective is always more or less suspicious and very inquisitive." Nathan Shapiro follows the rules, although with no special hope that, in his case, much will come of it. It is Shapiro's belief that he is good only with a gun. That much he will admit.

He went back, a little reluctantly, and sat down and sipped his sweet wine. It did taste rather syrupy. Rose looked at him, dark eyes intent. He put the glass down and nodded his head.

"I'm afraid it is your kid, darling," Nathan told his wife. "Blond boy? Good-looking? Eighteen or thereabouts?"

"Yes."

"Athlete? Track, maybe?"

"I think so. He's a good student, Nathan. Mr. Pierson — he has Roy in a creative writing class — thinks the boy has unusual talent. And — he's a good boy. I know he's a good boy. It's some — some bad mistake."

Shapiro shook his head at that and took another sip from his glass and then said, "I'm afraid it doesn't look like being, Rose. You see, he was caught running and there was blood on his shirt. She was killed with a knife, Rose. Probably a switchblade like a good many of the kids carry. He didn't have it on him, but he had time to get rid of it. Probably they'll find it in the house somewhere. You say he and his father haven't much money?"

"I don't know," Rose said. "Don't really know. Only that his father's a grocery clerk or something like that."

"The boy had close to a hundred and fifty dollars in his pocket when they — the patrolman on the beat, actually — caught him running away from the house. He says he was running to find a policeman, but actually he ran away from one. He'd been working in Mrs. Singleton's garden. He says he does two afternoons a week and most of Sunday. The way it seems to figure —"

The way it seemed to figure was that Roy Baker thought the house was empty. He was right in part; both the cook and the maid were off on Sunday afternoons; Mrs. Singleton herself slept late on Sundays — on all days, presumably. On Sundays she had breakfast around eleven and after the cook had served it she was off for the day. Around two in the afternoon, or thereabouts, Mrs. Singleton went out to lunch, usually with friends.

Roy Baker, part-time gardener, general handy man when needed, would know the Sunday routine in the big house — the landmark duly certified by a commission. He admitted that he did. He denied he knew that Jennifer was inclined casually to drop money into an unlocked drawer in her dressing table — money the maid and the cook could take for household expenses as they needed cash. He denied a lot of things without convincing anybody. He denied, specifically, murder. He denied that he had been looking for money, or anything else he could find, in Jennifer

19

Singleton's bedroom suite and had been walked in on by the woman he was stealing from and had attacked her with a knife, perhaps meaning only to threaten and killing when she ignored threats. Which would not make any difference in the outcome for the boy, since murder in the course of committing a felony is murder in the first degree.

Why had he run to find a policeman instead of telephoning?

He had thought whoever killed Mrs. Singleton might have left his fingerprints on the telephone.

"Which," Shapiro said, "is about as thin as they come, Rose."

"He's a boy," she said. "A frightened boy. Thinking like a terrified boy. The money?"

"He says that part of it was his wages for the week, which was in an envelope on the kitchen table, where it usually was left for him on Sundays. The rest — a hundred dollars — he said was a present from Mrs. Singleton. A graduation present. It was in a separate envelope with his name on it. He said he had gone upstairs, after calling up and not being answered, and knocked on the door to her rooms. He says he wanted to thank her. He said the door was not tightly shut and that when he knocked he knocked it open. He says he said, 'Mrs. Singleton?' and then saw her lying face down on the floor. He says he turned her over on her back, thinking that she was merely hurt, and that that must have been when he got blood on his skivvy shirt."

"It could have been that way," Rose said. "Nathan, it *was* that way. You don't listen. You've known me a long time and you know who I am. What I'm like. But you don't listen."

"To you," Shapiro said, "I always listen, darling. You think he's the kind of boy who wouldn't do a thing like this. But it isn't that easy, Rose. Be fine if it were — if we could just look at somebody and maybe talk to him a little and then say, 'Yeah, he's a killer, all right,' or 'Nope, not the type to kill anybody.' Make police work a lot —"

"Don't tell me what I already know," Rose said. "It isn't like you."

"Still?" Nathan Shapiro said, his voice soft, "what you say does come to that, doesn't it? That you can tell what a person is, and is capable of, by looking at him. Talking to him."

"Not everybody," Rose said. "I don't say that. But — he's a kid, Nathan. I know kids. . Good kids and stubborn kids. When you see as many as I've seen for a long time you get — oh, feelings about them. You see the same traits appear and reappear. Some girls are going to turn out to be tramps, and you rec-

21

ognize trampishness in a girl before she really begins to show it. Some boys — mostly the stupid ones, but not always — are going to get in worse and worse trouble the older they get."

"Predestination?"

"No. Oh, a lot of things. Environment. It's bad for a lot of kids at Clayton High. For a lot of kids all through the city. Resentment. Anger. A lot of things that a lot of people think explain everything. They do explain a lot. But there's something left over, Nate. Something that — oh, that's built into people."

"Genes?"

"All right," Rose said. "Call it genes. Call it whatever you want to. Roy Baker wouldn't steal and he wouldn't kill. I — oh, I know what you're going to say. I can't prove it. Call it anything you want to. Call it a woman's intuition."

"No," Shapiro said; "even I stop at some things, dear. You're a good character witness. Qualified beyond most." He smiled at her. "In most things, come to that," Nathan Shapiro said.

He waited a moment for her to smile back at him. After a moment she did smile.

"It's as much your job as arresting people," Rose said. "As much your job to see that the wrong people aren't arrested. Isn't it?"

"It's not my case. Precinct thinks they've got it sewed up. Two men from the squad are sitting in, and by the time they get on the squad they're good men." He paused and his long face lengthened. "With exceptions," he said.

"You," Rose Shapiro told her husband, "are impossible."

This seemed to please him. She's a very reassuring woman, Shapiro thought. She's discerning about many things. She will never admit, even to herself, that she is not discerning about me.

"Come out of it," Rose said. "Remember, I told you once you are very like your father. Look at your father, Nate."

A portrait of Rabbi Shapiro was above the fireplace. It was not a particularly good portrait. It was a portrait of a man with a long face and brooding dark eyes. It's just, Nathan Shapiro thought, that I look a little like him. He was a wise and gentle man and because I look a little like him it throws her off. I'm a cop who is handy with a gun.

"All right," Shapiro said, "in the morning I'll talk to Bill Weigand. I'll tell him my wife knows this kid didn't kill anybody and that precinct's wrong and the assistant district attorney who's sitting in doesn't know which end is up. All right?"

"Very much all right," Rose said. "Turn on the symphony, Nathan."

He turned on the radio, but he didn't really listen to Beethoven. He somewhat preferred Brahms, as a matter of fact. But even from Brahms, he realized, his mind would have wandered. A kid in shock could run out and look for a cop, instead of using the telephone. It is difficult to tell what a frightened kid will do.

Shapiro sat at his desk and read reports. They did not add much to what Tony Cook had told him on the telephone. Patrolman Williams (J. K.) had been "proceeding" through Point Street and had seen a boy run out of the house at No. 278. The boy had run toward the east, which would have taken him to Seventh Avenue. (Where, to be sure, he might have found a traffic cop.) He had stopped when hailed; had gone willingly enough back into the house with Patrolman Williams — gone up wide stairs to the second floor and led the way into two rear rooms, with a bath between them, which stretched the sixty-foot width of the house. They had found the body of Jennifer Singleton, face up, on a soft rug which had once been pale yellow and which wasn't any longer. Williams had used the tele-

24

phone — a white telephone on a small table with a glass top.

Williams had seen no disorder in the room when he first went into it; he had seen only a dead woman who had been beautiful — a woman with a wide, unlined forehead and very large blue eyes set far apart and with light brown hair which seemed to shine. She had been a little woman. When she died she had been wearing a blue silk suit, the jacket open over a white blouse. The wound, which Williams thought had been made with a knife, was just under her left breast. The body was still warm. When an assistant medical examiner made his guess some forty-five minutes later, it was that Jennifer Singleton had been dead not much more than an hour.

At the Charles Street station house the boy had told his story. During several hours of questioning, he had stuck to his story. A man from the Homicide Bureau of the District Attorney's office had sat in on the questioning; Detectives Stevens and Altgelt from Homicide South had joined precinct detectives.

The boy said he had gone upstairs to thank Mrs. Singleton for his graduation present and knocked at a partly closed door and the door had opened far enough for him to see her lying on the floor. He had thought at first that she had fallen; only when, calling her name, he had turned her on her back had he seen the deep, still bleeding wound in her chest. He had not used the telephone because he had read about fingerprints and knew better than to touch anything.

He had been pretty sure she was dead. Because there was so much blood. Yes, blood was still coming out of the wound, but not very fast.

No, he did not know that she had been in the habit of tossing money, loose, into a drawer of her dressing table so that Maria Gomez, the maid, and Mrs. Florinda James, the cook, could take out what they needed for incidental expenses connected with the operation of the house. There was no money in the drawer when the police looked into it.

The money in his pocket was his own. He had worked fourteen hours that week — four hours on Tuesday and again on Thursday; six hours that Sunday. Tuesday he had cleaned out the basement; Thursday and Sunday he had worked in the garden. She paid him two dollars and a half an hour.

His wages, then, came to thirty-five dollars. Most of the rest was a present of a hundred dollars. The wages had been in one envelope, left on the kitchen table where it usually was on Sundays, and the present in another envelope, with the words "Graduation Gift" written on it. He had put both envelopes in the kitchen trash can after he had taken the money out of them. Because the trash can was full, and because he knew that Mrs. James was off on Sunday afternoons, he had emptied it in the incinerator. He usually did that on Sundays.

Yes, he knew — anyway he supposed — that Maria Gomez was off that afternoon too.

He hadn't, until he went upstairs and called and knocked on the door, known whether Mrs. Singleton was home or not. If she wasn't, he had meant to write "Thank you for the wonderful present" on a sheet of paper from her desk.

He had never owned a switchblade knife in his life — or borrowed one from any of the other kids. Yes, he knew that some of the kids had switchblades. Actually, he didn't own any kind of a knife. Sure he knew where the kitchen knives were kept.

He hadn't killed anybody. Mrs. Singleton was a lovely lady. A wonderful lady.

He hadn't seen Patrolman Williams when he ran out of the house. He didn't have eyes in the back of his head. If he had seen the patrolman he would have told him what had happened. He was running to find a policeman, not to get away from one. Almost always there was a traffic policeman at Seventh Avenue and Greenwich.

They had got in touch with the boy's father, who was Ralph Baker and was in his two-room apartment on the fourth floor of a tenement house in Morton Street. They had got other clothes for the boy from his father. The clothes Roy had been wearing to work in Mrs. Singleton's garden were by then evidence, not clothing to be worn.

There was blood on the white skivvy shirt. There was also blood on the denim trousers. Blood spurts when the aorta is sliced open.

He had been booked as a material witness. The man from the D.A.'s Homicide Bureau had authorized a homicide charge, but there was no hurry about that.

The boy had been told he could make a telephone call and that he was entitled to have a lawyer if he wanted one. He had been crying then. He had said he didn't know any lawyer to call. He had been offered food and shaken his head, still crying. He had been locked up.

Probably by now, Nathan Shapiro thought when he had finished with the reports, he's been arraigned in felony court and bound over for the grand jury. And a hundred to one he'll be indicted, charge felony murder. And a hundred to one, again, they won't let him cop a plea. What it comes to, they've got him cold. Rose has identified herself with a no-good kid.

He buzzed the cubbyhole office of Captain

William Weigand, commanding, Homicide South. Bill Weigand said, "Right, Nate. Come along." Nathan Shapiro went along, feeling even more than usually dismal about everything. He sat down opposite Weigand's desk and said, "This Singleton kill, Captain."

"A hell of a thing," Bill Weigand said. "One hell of a thing, Nate. She was one of the great ones. Must have been — oh, somewhere in her middle fifties. Maybe older than that. And she could make you think her thirty years younger. And some snot-nose kid, trying to steal a hundred bucks or so —"

He spread his hands hopelessly. He said, "What the hell's the matter with these kids, Nate?"

"I've been reading the reports," Shapiro said. "Looks bad for the kid."

"It's wrapped up," Weigand said. But then he looked intently at Nathan Shapiro for some seconds and said, "It's not your baby, Nate. Not ours, really. You know what some of the precinct squads call us, Nate. The brain boys. No need for the brain boys this time."

"Way it looks," Shapiro said.

"Right," Bill Weigand said. "So — time heavy on your hands, Nate? Now you've wrapped up the Mathewson kill?"

"This boy," Shapiro said, "goes to the school my wife's assistant principal of. Clayton

29

High. On Greenwich."

"I know that," Weigand told him. "How is Rose, by the way?"

"That's the point, Bill," Nathan Shapiro said. "She's upset. About this kid she's upset. You see, she thinks he's a fine boy. Not a boy who would kill anybody."

Bill Weigand looked briefly at the ceiling. Then he looked at Nate Shapiro.

"She knows him pretty well?" Weigand said. "There are — God knows — hundreds of kids at Clayton."

"She says he stands out," Shapiro said. "Seems he does, in a way. Member of the student council and that sort of thing. One of his teachers thinks he's a brilliant kid."

"Nate," Weigand said, "the precinct boys think they've got him cold. The assistant district attorney thinks they've get him cold. Steven and Altgelt sat in for a while last night and they think it's pinned on him and pinned tight. Right?"

"The way it reads," Shapiro said.

"And Rose thinks different," Weigand said.

"She thinks different, Bill. And she knows a lot about kids. She's known one hell of a lot of kids. All kinds. She's good with kids, Bill."

"So," Weigand said, "you want to play Rose's hunch, Nate? Look. I know her. She's quite a person, this Rose of yours. All right, she knows about kids. But —" He stopped and again consulted the ceiling, this time for more than a minute. Then he said, "She's sold you this hunch of hers, Nate?"

"Enough to make me wonder."

"Long time ago," Weigand said, "I learned not to look gift hunches in the teeth. Get on with your wondering, Nate. If something hot breaks I'll probably have to call you off it. You want somebody with you?"

"Tony Cook's a useful sort of guy."

"Right," Weigand said. "You and Cook go wondering for a couple of days."

III

Start with the hunch that it wasn't as simple as it looked; start with a hunch which wasn't even his own. Which meant start at the end, which had been the end of a middle-aged woman named Jennifer Singleton who had been a celebrated actress. Start at the end and work back to the beginning. Which meant, among other things, working back through Jennifer Singleton's life to find out if there was somebody who, because of something which had happened in her life, wanted her dead.

He'd grope and grope, Shapiro thought, leaving Weigand's office for the squad room, beckoning Anthony Cook from his desk, and the chances were a hundred to one nothing would come of it. It is, Shapiro thought, a kind of groping for which I am singularly ill equipped. Johnny Stein, now — Johnny probably knows his way among people who live in the theater. Only they've transferred Johnny to Homicide North.

"You know anything about this Mrs. Singleton?" Shapiro asked Tony Cook and Cook looked at him with some surprise and said, "Who doesn't, Nate?"

Nathan Shapiro said that he didn't; said that sure he had heard her name; had seen advertisements in which her name was in larger type than the name of the play she was in and in type many times larger than that of the man or woman who had written the play.

"I don't know," Cook said, "they say she was great. I saw her in a couple of plays — one about five years ago and last week in the one she's in now; was in. I guess maybe she was great." He paused. "This thing she's in now," Tony Cook said. "Was in. Rachel made a pitch about seeing it. Rachel Farmer."

"Yes," Shapiro said, "I know the Rachel you mean, Tony. How is this Rachel of yours?"

"Not mine," Tony said. "Not yet. Anyhow, not the way you mean. She's fine. So we went to this play. Called *Always Good-bye,* the play is. About a woman who —"

"All right, Tony," Shapiro said. "You saw the play. Mrs. Singleton had an important part in it, I gather?"

"Put it this way," Tony Cook said. "She *was* it. This woman, you see, has a lot of men crazy about her and —"

33

"Yes," Shapiro said. "Tell me another time, Tony. You thought she was good? Very good?"

"O.K.," Tony said. "She was a knockout. Says on the reports she was in her fifties somewhere. Maybe almost sixty. Hell, she looked being maybe thirty. And damn good-looking. And she had a voice like nobody's I've ever heard and when she laughed — she had a sort of low laugh like — hell, I don't know. Like water running over stones in a brook. Know what I mean?"

"I guess so," Shapiro said. "I guess maybe."

"So you wanted to laugh too," Cook said. "Even when there wasn't anything specially funny. Another thing, Nate. When she was on-stage it was like there wasn't anybody else on it. I mean, they were all right. Most of the time, anyway. It wasn't as if she wanted them to disappear or anything like that. It was just that — oh, when she came on, everything kind of lighted up. Know what I mean?"

"I guess so, Tony."

"So," Cook said, "what's the pitch, Lieutenant? This kid killed her when he was looking for what was worth grabbing and she walked in on him."

"Way it looks," Nathan Shapiro said, sadly and thinking that it sure as hell did. "Seems, though, the captain isn't entirely satisfied. You know the way he is, Tony. Doesn't want to take any chances we're wrong."

Which was true enough, at least in general.

"So," Shapiro said, "he wants us to look around. Just to be sure there aren't any loose ends anywhere. So suppose you see what you can dig up about the lady, Tony. If she's as well known as she seems to have been, she'd be in *Who's Who,* maybe."

"There's something called *Who's Who in the Theatre,*" Cook said. "Anyway, I think there is."

"Maybe," Shapiro said, "you can find somebody who knew her pretty well and —"

"Wait a minute," Cook said. "Slip came through a little while ago. Seems some man showed up around six-thirty last night, while the boys were still there. Seems he had a dinner date with Mrs. Singleton. Wait a minute."

They had walked as they talked, and were in a corridor outside the squad room. Cook went back and Shapiro waited. Cook came back. "Man named Lester Agee," Cook said, and spelled the last name out. "Report says, 'Agee expressed shock at news of Mrs. Singleton's death.' Wait a minute."

Shapiro waited.

"Seems to me," Cook said, "I've seen that name somewhere. Out-of-the-way name, sort of."

He tapped the side of his head with finger tips, as if his memory was a stopped clock which needed starting up.

"Got it," Cook said. "He's the guy wrote this play she was in. Could be he'll know about her."

"Yes," Shapiro said. "And probably she had an agent. Understand actors and people like that do have them."

"Flesh peddlers," Cook said. "That's what they call them. O.K., Lieutenant. I'll dig around. Catch up with you where?"

"I'll be downtown," Shapiro said. "Lunch down there some place."

"Rachel and I —" Cook said, and stopped. "Sometimes when I'm down that way, Nate, I go to a little Italian joint. Just a joint, but it's O.K."

He named the little joint and gave Shapiro its address.

"When we can make it," Shapiro said. "Unless something comes up."

"You'll be?"

"Well," Shapiro said, "I'll probably go back to school, Tony."

Shapiro took a downtown Seventh Avenue local and got off at the Sheridan Square station and climbed stairs into bewilderment. From Sheridan Square, which is not a square, streets seemed to go off in all directions. He should, he thought, have brought Tony Cook along as a guide. Tony's girl lived down here some-where — Tony's thin dark girl who so often posed naked for painters that she didn't, half the time, seem to know whether she had any clothes on or not. Or, for that matter, care.

There was a traffic policeman in the middle of the maze of streets which converged at, and crossed, Seventh Avenue. When the lights were in his favor — Nathan Shapiro crosses only with the green — he got to the traffic cop. The cop told him that the Clayton High School was on Greenwich, which Shapiro al-ready knew, and where Greenwich was, which Shapiro hadn't known. Point Street was an-other matter. The traffic cop had to think that one out.

When he had, he said that Point Street wasn't really a street. Point Street was a block of a street which was called Van Allen, and why the hell it was called Point Street for that single block the cop sure as hell didn't know, Lieutenant. The best way to get to that block, he guessed, was to —

Shapiro listened carefully, learned by rote. He went, he hoped, as directed. He got lost only briefly — came to Van Allen and walked west through it, looking at street signs. (The most prominent signs said "One Way," but Shapiro was used to that. Most of the streets in Manhattan are named "One Way," now and then with no other visible designation.) On one side of an intersection, Shapiro was walking west through Van Allen Street. On the other side he walked through Point Street.

No. 278 would be on the south side of the street. It was, in mid-block. It was made the easier to find because there was a police cruise car parked in front of it. It was a wide brick house, expansive by comparison with the houses which abutted it on either side. It had a wide double door under a pointed arch. Both doors had leaded panes. Three white steps led up to the doors. When Shapiro went up them, one of the doors opened and a thin man in a dark suit, and with a hat on, said, "Looking for somebody, mister?"

"Homicide," Shapiro said and gave his name. He didn't hesitate over the "Lieutenant" part of it. He merely lowered his voice a little.

"Don't know what you'll find, sir," the precinct detective said. "We're looking for the knife this kid used."

"Find it?"

They hadn't found it yet. They'd only been at it half an hour or so. Had to be around somewhere, because the kid hadn't had it on him when he was picked up and hadn't had much chance to throw it away outside. Been in sight from the time he ran out of the house, and the cop who picked him up was pretty sure he hadn't thrown anything away.

Shapiro went into a narrow room with a polished floor and a wide staircase mounting from the end of it. The staircase had rails as polished as the shining floor. At either side of the narrow room there were archways, giving access to high-ceilinged rooms. In one of the rooms, that on the right as Shapiro stood facing the staircase, two men were turning over cushions of chairs, removing books from low shelves and putting them back again.

The second floor, the reports had said. Shapiro went up the stairs, which had been built for the comfort of those who used them — built with wide treads, short risers. There was room in this old house for an easy, elegant staircase. When the house was built — Shapiro could not guess how long ago — there had been no need to pinch space in.

At the top of the stairs there was a wide hallway. On either side of the main staircase, lesser staircases led to higher floors. Across the corridor, opposite the head of the main staircase, there were two closed oak doors.

"One on the left isn't locked," the precinct man said up the stairs. "Happened in the bedroom."

Shapiro went in — went into a carpeted

room with windows which reached from ceiling to floor and opened, although now they were not open, onto a narrow balcony with a wrought-iron railing.

There was a fireplace of marble in the room, and a sofa faced it — a low sofa, upholstered in yellow brocade. There were two other, smaller, sofas in the big room and one was white and the other yellow, but a deeper yellow than the big sofa in front of the fireplace. A white silk fan, flecked with gold, spread in the fireplace opening.

There was a small white desk, delicately designed, in a corner of the room. There was serenity in the room which had, evidently, been Jennifer Singleton's upstairs sitting room, although probably she had called it something else. Drawing room? Shapiro didn't know. He walked across the room to one of the windows, through which morning sun slanted.

He looked down into a garden, and the garden was bright with flowers. Shapiro did not know what flowers they were. (When there were flowers blooming in Prospect Park they had names assigned to them; names on cards atop metal spikes stuck into the ground.)

The garden he looked down into, on the south side of this expanded house, had flagstone paths running through it, and at the far end — where the garden ended in a board fence with flowers (bright, sprawling flowers) painted on it — there was a fountain with a white statue of a naked boy shining in it.

The garden, to Shapiro's entirely inexperienced eyes, looked immaculate. The soil between the plants looked — he searched his mind for a word. Looked granulated . . . "cultivated." That was the word for gardens. The flags which formed paths had obviously been swept. Moss was green between the stones.

The garden stretched the width of the house, which was, he guessed, sixty feet or more. The kid had kept the garden neat.

Shapiro left the window and found the hallway which led from this room to the next. Off the hallway was a bathroom, and it was a great deal of bathroom. It had a sunken tub big enough to swim in. There was a dressing table built into one wall; there were enough fresh yellow towels on racks to dry a multitude. Shapiro went on into Jennifer Singleton's bedroom, which was the room she had died in.

It was not as large as the first room he had gone into, and this, he realized, was because one end of it was a wall of sliding doors. He slid one of them open and looked in at clothes — gay clothes impertinent on hangers. He had never seen so many clothes. He had, as he looked around the room, seldom seen so wide and low a bed. It jutted from the inner wall, toward the windows — windows not as deep as in the other room. At the foot of the bed was a radio-television combination. Under the windows was a dressing table with a long mirror over it. There were light tubes along both sides, and along the top of the mirror.

Between radio-television combination and dressing-table bench there was an oval, fluffy rug. It had been pale yellow. It was not any longer. Blood had soaked into it.

Shapiro opened the door beside the head of the bed and went into the outside hallway. He stood in the doorway and looked into the bedroom.

He could see the stained yellow rug. If there had been the body of a woman lying on it he could have seen the body. As Roy Baker said he had seen it. Which wasn't, of course, much of anything to go on. The kid had worked in the house. He knew the lay of it.

He hadn't, Shapiro thought, going down the shallow staircase, learned very much. Jennifer Singleton had lived graciously, in the elegance of this landmark mansion — this big house which, since it had been so designated by the Landmarks Preservation Commission, could not be externally altered. (There had been plenty of alterations inside, obviously; whoever had built it, whenever that had been, had certainly not built so much closet space into it or installed a small swimming pool for a bathtub. And probably, then, houses had not abutted the big house. Probably there had been open lawns around it.)

Jennifer Singleton had lived gracefully. A boy named Roy Baker had kept her garden immaculate. There had been nothing either graceful or immaculate about the manner of her death. Her body could have been seen from a doorway if a door, not latched shut, opened when a boy knocked on it.

But precinct knew all that. The room had been photographed; the room had been measured and a plan of it had been sketched. Nathan Shapiro had learned nothing new, which was as he had expected. He went down the wide, shallow stairway, which, he supposed, very elegant ladies had descended a hundred years ago.

"Find anything we didn't find, Lieutenant?" the man from the precinct squad asked him, a little too politely. Shapiro said he hadn't. He said, "Find the knife yet?"

They had not found a switchblade knife. The kitchen knives looked clean, but there were three or four of a size to match the wound. Those would go to the lab. A murderer in a hurry cannot be sure he has washed a knife clean of blood. The lab could make sure.

Shapiro went out of the big house and down the three immaculately white steps. He went, he hoped, toward Greenwich Avenue and the Clayton High School. He only got lost twice, neither time hopelessly.

The high school was new and very modern. There was a great deal of glass in windows which could not be opened. There was a playground adjacent to the school and lines were painted on the cement surface, marking off courts for various games. The lines crossed one another, to Shapiro bewilderingly. But probably the kids weren't bewildered. There were no kids in sight. Shapiro went into the school, which was pleasantly air-conditioned but still smelled a little like a school. There was a counter with a young woman behind it.

"Mrs. Shapiro, if she's free," Mrs. Shapiro's husband said.

The young woman didn't know. Who wished to see Mrs. Shapiro?

"Tell her the police," Shapiro said and was looked at with astonishment. "Represented," Shapiro said, "by a lieutenant from Homicide South."

The young woman used a telephone. She said, "Your wife's free, Lieutenant Shapiro. Down that way."

He went that way. He went past a door marked: "Principal." He came to a door marked: "Assistant Principal" and knocked on it, and Rose said, "Come in, Nathan."

The office was small, but the desk Rose sat behind was not. She was trim in a dark blue dress with white collar and cuffs. She looked as if she belonged behind the big desk. It is odd, Shapiro thought, how many aspects there can be to one small woman with large dark eyes. She never used much lipstick but now he was not sure she was wearing any. Not that it mattered with her mouth.

"Nathan," Rose Shapiro said. "You did talk to Bill Weigand, then?"

"As instructed," Nathan said, gravely. "And, yes, my dear, he told me to poke around. Because you have a hunch."

He felt slightly that the "my dear" had been a mistake. Perhaps "Madam Principal"?

"You told him that?"

"I had to tell him something. Everybody is satisfied with what they've got. What do you know about Jennifer Singleton, Rose?"

"What everybody knows. A — oh, a great lady of the American stage, to use a bromide. With a theater named after her. And that as soon as she agrees to star — agreed to star — in a play it became a vehicle. You didn't come here to ask me that, Nathan."

45

"To find out what I can about this kid," Shapiro said. "Find out what makes him tick, if anybody knows what makes him tick. His teachers might, I thought."

Momentarily, a vertical thought line appeared between Rose Shapiro's dark eyebrows. She said, "Umm." She said, "Most of our classes are very large, Nathan. Much too large. It's hard for even a good teacher — and most of ours are pretty dedicated people or they wouldn't work for the salaries they get — hard for even a good teacher to get to know the pupils as individuals. Really to know them."

"Last night," Shapiro said, "you mentioned one teacher who thinks young Baker is a brilliant boy. That was the word you used, I think. A man named — what was it? Perkins?"

"Pierson," Rose said. "Has Roy in an English class. 'Creative writing,' it's called. And, yes, Nathan, it's a small class, as our classes go. A lot of our kids don't get, or want to get, much above creative spelling. You want to talk to Mr. Pierson?"

"A place to start," Shapiro said. "Yes, I'd like to."

She used the telephone on her desk. She said, "Oh, Molly. Send a monitor to Mr. Pierson's classroom, please. Have the monitor say I'd like to see him in my office." She lis-

46

tened for a moment. "I know," she said. "Tell him it probably won't be for long. His pupils can write creatively in his absence." She put the receiver back in its cradle. "If ever," she added.

The telephone rang. She said "Mrs. Shapiro" into it and then, "Of course, Mr. Cunningham. In — will five minutes be all right?" A man's voice shuffled out of the receiver, as voices shuffle out of telephones. "In five minutes, then," Rose said.

Almost at once somebody knocked on the office door. Rose said, "Come in," and a thin small man came in. He was a little stooped and his fair hair was more than a little thin. He said, "You wanted to see me, Mrs. Shapiro? I hope there's nothing —"

"It's about Roy Baker, Mr. Pierson," Rose said. "This is Lieutenant Shapiro of the police."

Pierson looked at her and then looked at Nathan Shapiro. He looked away from each of them quickly. A tentative little man, Shapiro thought, with sympathy.

"Yes," Rose said, "we're related, Mr. Pierson. By marriage."

She got up from behind her desk. She said, "Mr. Cunningham wants to see me. If that doesn't take too long, I'll go along to your class, Mr. Pierson, and keep them out of mischief."

When she had gone, Shapiro went to sit behind her desk. He felt slightly like a usurper. He said, "Sit down, Professor Pierson."

"Mister," Pierson said, and sat down.

"You've heard about young Baker?" Shapiro asked.

"I find it hard to believe," Pierson said. He had a light voice. "He has always seemed a fine young man. A most promising boy."

"Brilliant, my wife says you think him, Mr. Pierson."

"Potentially," Pierson said. "Potentially, Lieutenant."

"My wife," Shapiro said, "probably doesn't know him as well as you do. But she is quite sure that he isn't the kind of boy who would do what he appears to have done. What the evidence indicates he has done. You agree?"

"Entirely," Pierson said. "He's always seemed a fine young man. Outstanding. That he would harm anyone — let alone Jennifer — well, I find it almost impossible to believe. Of course —"

His light voice trailed off. Shapiro waited. Then he said, "Of course what, Mr. Pierson?"

"One doesn't know, does one?" Pierson said. "I mean, what others are capable of? It is easy to be wrong about people, I'm afraid."

"It often is," Shapiro said. "You feel now

you may have been wrong about Roy Baker? That he isn't a fine young man who wouldn't harm anyone?"

"No," Pierson said. "Oh, no. Only that one can never be entirely certain. You do say the evidence points to him?"

"At the moment," Shapiro said. "He's being questioned. He denies killing Mrs. Singleton, of course. Says she was dead, or dying, when he found her. Is he a truthful boy, Mr. Pierson? Not that we'd expect him to admit he killed the woman. But, in general, truthful?"

Pierson had "always found him so."

"Not unruly in any way? Tough? Some of the kids are nowadays. Not that some of them weren't always."

Not that Pierson knew of. Certainly never in class. But he added to that. "Of course," he said, "I've known him only during the past two semesters, Lieutenant. The creative writing class is for seniors. So are the other advanced English classes I teach. What he was like his first three years here I don't really know."

"Since you have had him in your classes, a good student? And, I take it, a well-behaved one?"

"Oh, yes."

"And a boy with talent. Happen to know anything about his background, Mr. Pierson?"

Pierson didn't really. He understood the boy's mother was dead and that his father was a clerk somewhere — at, he thought, some store in the Village.

He wasn't getting much of anywhere, Shapiro thought. Except that Pierson was hedging a bit; wasn't going out on a limb for the boy. Which was probably Pierson's tentative way in many things.

"By the way," Shapiro said. "When you spoke of the late Mrs. Singleton you called her Jennifer. As if you knew her."

"People do that," Pierson said. "About theater people. Tallulah. Ethel. Not to their faces, of course." He paused for a moment. "As a matter of fact," he said, "I did know Mrs. Singleton slightly. That is, I'd met her."

Shapiro did not show the slight surprise he felt. He would have expected the gap between Jennifer Singleton and this small, tentative schoolteacher to be wide indeed.

"We're trying, of course," Shapiro said, "to find out every thing we can about Mrs. Singleton. Talk to as many people as we can who knew her at all."

"I can't," Pierson said, "really say I knew her. I met her — oh, a couple of times. At parties. Was introduced to her, anyway. Probably if she were alive and you asked her if she'd ever met a man named Clarke Pierson

50

she'd just look blank. People like me remember meeting people like her. Not the other way around."

Which seemed likely to Nathan Shapiro. But if you see the most insignificant of loose threads you pull at it. He pulled at this one. He said, "These parties. Theatrical parties? I mean parties at which there were people from the theater."

"You wonder how I'd go to a party like that, don't you, Lieutenant? Doesn't seem probable to you, does it?"

"Doesn't seem any special way," Shapiro said.

"There's no secret about it," Clarke Pierson said. "And nothing that would be useful in your investigation. Four years ago I wrote a play. An unwary producer put it on. On Broadway. It opened on a Tuesday evening and closed the next Saturday. I ran into theater people while we were getting it ready to flop. All pleasant and hopeful until it did."

"And went to parties with them."

"As I said, once or twice. All right — one of the guys I ran into was a playwright named Agee. Lester Agee. A very nice sort of person. Even dropped in at one of our previews. Made pleasant noises, although I suppose he knew better. His plays don't flop."

"Agee," Shapiro said. "Didn't he write the

51

play Mrs. Singleton has been appearing in?"

"Yes," Pierson said. "Big hit. Chiefly because she was starred in it. It's — oh, it's a rather obvious play. Good enough theater with Jennifer in it. Nothing without her — nothing much, anyway. Written for her, at a guess. Close without her, pretty certainly."

"Written for her?"

"With her in mind. He'd written others for her, you know. At least one before they were married. Vehicle sort of thing, but she was good in it. Ran a couple of years, actually. And another while they were still married. Comedy, although Jennifer wasn't really very good at comedy. Ran a season, all the same."

Get him on the theater and he talks, Shapiro thought. Not, probably, to my purpose.

"You still writing plays, Mr. Pierson?"

"No. A lesson learned, Lieutenant. Now I teach the young how to be creative. Another way of wasting time, I sometimes think, but there's a salary goes with it. Speaking of the not-so-creative young —"

He looked across the desk at Shapiro and raised pale eyebrows. He put his hands on the arms of the chair.

"Realize I'm taking up your time," Shapiro said. "We have to bother a lot of people in a thing like this. Appreciate what you've told me about young Baker."

Pierson stood up.

"Getting back to him," Shapiro said. "Any idea how he got this job with Mrs. Singleton?"

"We try here at the school," Pierson said, "to help kids who want part-time jobs — after-school jobs. Saturday and Sunday jobs. We hear of somebody who wants a kid we tell a kid about it, if there's one on the list seems suitable."

"It's generally known you have this list of kids looking for jobs?"

"I suppose so," Pierson said. "I don't know much about it. Or whether Roy was recommended by us to Mrs. Singleton. Miss Cudahay might know. She's on the front desk."

Shapiro thanked him and said he'd been a help, which Shapiro did not think particularly true. Clarke Pierson wisped his way out of the office.

IV

Walking Greenwich Village streets again in search of the restaurant — the joint — Tony Cook had named to him, Nathan Shapiro did not really get lost. He merely, as he realized later, went considerably out of his way. He walked through Eighth Street, among oddly dressed young people of assorted colors and most of them noticeably hairy. One could tell the males from the females for the most part. The boys had hair on their faces, as well as down the backs of their necks.

At Fifth he walked south and through the Square. Beyond it he found the street he was looking for and, after passing it once, the restaurant. It was down three steps from street level and, inside, it smelled of garlic. Tony Cook was at a corner table in the rear of the narrow room, talking up to a man in a white apron — a very fresh white apron. Tony Cook had a cocktail glass in front of him. He raised it in greeting to Nathan Shapiro, who went gloomily down the room, sympathizing in advance with his stomach, which was going to be displeased. It often is.

The man in the white apron beamed at him. Introduced — he was Nicholas Gazzi — he shook hands heartily and said, "Can I get you something from the bar, Lieutenant?"

"Sherry," Shapiro said, and sat down. Nick Gazzi looked somewhat doubtful. "Only domestic, Lieutenant," Nick said. "A nice glass of chianti, maybe? Or a martini, yes?"

"Domestic sherry'll be all right," Shapiro said.

"Be on the sweet side, probably," Tony Cook said. "They make pretty good martinis, Lieutenant."

"Sherry," Shapiro said. "I don't mind if it's sweet."

Nick Gazzi shrugged resigned shoulders and went up the room to a small bar near the door. There were two men sitting at the bar and, at a corner table from which, looking up, they could see the legs of people walking outside, two women, one in a severe suit and the other in a flowered dress.

"Busier at night," Cook said. "Even got a man plays the piano. You don't look very happy about the morning, Nate."

"Lieutenant" was reserved for more formal moments.

"Not especially," Shapiro said and "Thank

55

you," to Nick Gazzi for a wineglass of dark brown fluid. Shapiro tasted it. It was sweet, all right. Gazzi said, "Please," which didn't seem to mean anything, and went out through swinging doors at the rear of the dining room.

"Mrs. Singleton's house is quite something," Shapiro said. "The boy took good care of her garden. The boy could, as he says, have seen her body from the door of her bedroom, if it opened when he knocked on it. At the school, everybody spoke well of the kid and nobody believed he would kill anybody."

"Come to that," Cook said, "nobody ever does. Most of the time, anyway."

"The kid," Shapiro said, "got his job with Mrs. Singleton through a kind of employment office the school runs for kids who want part-time jobs. A man named Gage called up for Mrs. Singleton. They sent three boys over and she turned down the first two and took Roy Baker on. Last October, that was. To clean up her garden for the winter. She kept him on through the winter, doing odd jobs — there'd be plenty in a house as big as hers. Apparently he was a good worker."

"Also," Cook said, "from what they say he's a good-looking kid. I've an idea she liked good-looking kids around."

Shapiro merely raised his eyebrows.

"You said Gage," Tony Cook said. "The

man who called up for her?"

"Yes."

"He's her husband," Cook said. "Or widower. They were separated. Not divorced. Not yet, anyway. He's a good-looking kid, from his picture."

"Kid?"

"Maybe thirty," Cook said. "Kid by comparison. He's got a small part in this play she was in, *Always Good-bye.* Which is a hell of a hit, Nate. Has been since it opened last October. They were going to close it down during July and open up again in August. To give Mrs. Singleton — the others too, of course, but it was her idea — a vacation. They're pretty much sold out through next October. In a tizzy, Temple is."

"Temple?"

"The producer. Charles Temple. Very snappy guy, at the moment. Snapped at me. General idea seems to be if the police force was any good it wouldn't let people get killed. And producers of hit plays be inconvenienced by having to refund a hell of a lot of money."

"It will come to that, Tony?"

"What I gathered," Tony Cook said. "They don't say flat out but probably *Always Good-bye* is a dead duck without the lady. Because, like I said before, Nate, she was the play. She was this woman who —"

"Yes, Tony," Shapiro said. "You told me. Sounds as if you've had a busy morning."

"Sort of," Cook said, trying to remember if he had told Shapiro the story of the play. He couldn't remember that he had. He reached under his chair and came up with a large brown envelope. He opened it and took a glossy photograph out of it and laid it in front of Nathan Shapiro.

It was a photograph, artfully lighted, of a beautiful woman — a woman with wide-set eyes and high cheekbones. Her head had been a little raised for the photographer. The lines of jaw and chin were immaculately clean. There was a kind of sparkle, as well as beauty, in the pictured face.

"Our subject," Cook said, and watched Shapiro look at the photograph, lift it so that better light fell on it.

"Taken some time ago?" Shapiro said, and put the photograph down on the table and continued to look at it.

"Taken," Cook said, "just before the play opened. The play she was in, Nate. Taken last September, from what they say. What her publicity agent says. And, Nate, the way it figures she was damn near sixty. Fifty-eight anyway. If she told the truth in her *Who's Who* biog. Born 1910, it says. And — here's one for the book — born Jane Grumper. Want to eat or hear the rest of it?"

Tony Cook looked reflectively at his empty glass. He looked at Nathan Shapiro's, which was nearly empty.

"I'm not especially hungry," Shapiro said.

Cook was facing the little bar. He held up two fingers at the man behind it, who was not Nick Gazzi. The man said, "Right with you, Captain."

"Just a way he has of speaking," Cook said. "Knows I'm not a captain."

"Sure," Shapiro said. "Born Grumper. And?"

Born in September, 1910, daughter of Herman and Mary Grumper, in Milwaukee, Wisconsin. Educated, according to her biography in *Who's Who*, in Milwaukee public schools. Attended the University of Wisconsin. For Temple had told Cook, a year. Then she had come to New York and, for another year, studied acting at a dramatic school.

"She'd been in high-school plays, this Temple says," Cook told Shapiro, who sipped his sweet sherry and listened. "Been good in them. Was in one at the university, too. So —"

"She'd had gone a fall and a winter to the dramatic school; that summer she had got a part in a play which was trying out at a theater in the country. A producer saw it in the summer theater and liked it and put it on on Broadway.

"Wasn't much of a play, according to Temple," Cook said. "About a theatrical boarding house or something like that. Six girls in the cast, and Jane Grumper one of them. Only she wasn't calling herself Jane Grumper then. Jennifer Grenville, on account of Grumper —"

"Yes," Shapiro said. "I realize names make a difference, Tony."

The play had got tepid notices, according to Temple. But Jennifer Grenville hadn't. Of the half-dozen girls in the play — all pretty girls, according to Temple; all of them able to act a little — the reviewers had seemed to see only Jennifer. Temple had seen the play. He had told Cook, "This girl shone out of it. Even then, when she was just a kid, she had whatever it is some of them have. As if" — he had paused there, Cook told Nathan Shapiro — "as if there was a spot-light built into her. A light she carried with her."

"She got raves," Cook said. "A bit part, Temple called hers, and they raved about her."

The little play had run only a couple of months. Nobody remembered it after it had closed. But nobody ever forgot Jennifer Grenville. And Jennifer Grenville never went back to dramatic school. She went into another play, not in a bit part, and then, when that play's run ended, she married a man named Philip Singleton.

"Who," Cook said, "had one hell of a lot of money. And a family estate on Long Island somewhere and, for all I know, a couple of yachts. And Jennifer, while it lasted, gave up being an actress and spent her time being Mrs. Philip Singleton."

It had lasted a little over a year before Singleton, who was not as young as he liked to think himself, had a heart attack in the middle of a squash game and died of it.

"He left her one hell of a lot of money," Cook said. "A million, maybe. Maybe more. She could have spent the rest of her life twiddling her yachts."

She had not. Within a year after her husband's death, she had gone back to acting. She had kept the name of Singleton and grown famous under that name. She had had other names to sign checks with.

Three years after Singleton's death she had married an actor named Kurt Morton and that marriage had lasted for ten years and they had become famous as a team.

"Like the Lunts," Cook said. "Maybe more like Douglas Fairbanks and Mary Pickford. Seems to have been romantic as hell. Stories about their devoted marriage all over the place. Which, according to Temple, was great box-office. Starred together in four or five plays. And three of them were written by this guy Agee. The guy who was going to have taken her to dinner last night. The man who wrote this thing she was in until yesterday — this *Always Good-bye,* in which she played this woman who —"

"Yes, Tony," Shapiro said. "You told me. What happened to Morton?"

"The great romance went phfft," Cook said. "Surprised the hell out of everybody, Temple says. They'd been in a play together — a play Agee wrote for them — and Temple says they were great in it. He says there was amazing interplay between them always, whatever he means by that. And that he'd never seen it more — felt it more — than in that last play of theirs. The play ran two years and closed and they took the curtain bow together, like always, only this time they didn't just hold hands and bow. They held onto each other, Temple says."

"This man Temple seems to know a lot about her," Shapiro said and finished his sherry and waited, uneasily, to see what his stomach would make of it. It did not, immediately, comment.

"He was their producer by then," Cook said. "Was looking for another play for them for the next season. Only, she went to Reno. All very amicable, apparently. And six months after the divorce she married Agee. That lasted —"

"One thing at a time," Shapiro said. "What happened to Morton?"

"Never made it back, Temple says. Oh, had parts in other plays. But quit being a star. In some ways, according to Temple, he was a better actor than she was. Better at comedy, anyway. But she was the one who had what Temple calls the 'effulgence.' Whatever he means by that. He was dimmed out without her, according to —"

"Yes, Tony," Shapiro said. "I've got your man Temple straight. Very useful man to have dug up. This Kurt Morton still around?"

"Seems to be," Tony Cook said. "Spends most of his time at a club called The Players. Hasn't had a part for several years."

"Older than Mrs. Singleton?"

"No. Maybe five years younger. So's Agee, come to that. And as for young Gage —"

"The gentlemen care to order?" Nicholas Gazzi said, above them. "The lasagna I made myself." He put a thumb and a finger together and tossed them, together, into the air.

"Suits me," Cook said. "Damn good here, Nate."

"I wonder," Nathan Shapiro said, "if I could

have a chicken sandwich?"

"Chicken cacciatori," Gazzi said. "Wonderful." His thumb and finger performed again. "Spaghetti with meat sauce, maybe?"

"Just a chicken sandwich," Shapiro said.

Gazzi looked down at him with reproach, and shook his head in sorrow and surprise. But he said, "As you wish, sir," his tone formal. He went off shaking his head mournfully.

"He — Morton, I mean — seems to be the one who lost by the divorce," Shapiro said. "Her decision, you gather?"

"Seems to have been."

"Happen to know if they stayed friends? Or if he resented her going on without him? Going a long way, apparently."

That Tony Cook didn't know.

"All right," Shapiro said. "She married Agee. The man who was going to take her to dinner last night. How did that work out?"

"All right for maybe five years," Cook said. "Then she went to Reno again. But six months or so later she was back in another play of his. Made another big hit in it, Temple says. As big as she was having in *Always Goodbye,* which is about —"

"Yes," Shapiro said. "Apparently their professional association went along all right. You say he's younger than she was?"

"Maybe ten years younger, according to —"

"Yes," Shapiro said. "Who's young Gage, Tony?"

"The one she was still married to," Cook said. "Sort of, anyway. Compared to her, he's a kid. Maybe in his middle thirties, Temple says. Has a part in *Always Good-bye*. Not a big part."

" 'Sort of' married to her?"

"Well, he's got an apartment of his own in the Murray Hill area. Lived in this house of hers with her for about a year. Then moved into this apartment."

"Still married," Shapiro said. "Not working at it?"

"Sort of thing happens sometimes," Tony Cook said and, "Smells good as always, Nick," in response to an oval casserole of pasta. It smelled good to Shapiro, too. The chicken sandwich didn't smell much of anything except, faintly and inexplicably, of garlic.

"Still married," Shapiro said. "Still gets his legal share of whatever she left, doesn't he? From the looks of this house of hers, that could be quite a bit."

Tony Cook said what sounded a little like "gug." It is difficult to achieve clarity with a mouth full of lasagna. He swallowed. "Singleton left her a lot," he said. "She's been making a lot for years. And there's this, Nate. Temple doesn't know for sure, because apparently it was a private arrangement between her and Agee. But he thinks she was getting a cut of Agee's royalties. Which on a hit like *Always Good-bye* could add up."

It was conceivable, Nathan Shapiro thought, as he ate his sandwich and envied Anthony Cook his stomach, that there was quite a bit of addition to be undertaken. Not that it wasn't still, probably, the way it looked. It looked like being the kid, as it had from the start. Shapiro decided he might as well have a look at the kid.

V

The kid was still locked up in the Charles Street station house. And sure Lieutenant Shapiro could see him. There was a lack of enthusiasm in the voice and manner of the officer commanding the precinct detective squad.

"If you've got the time to waste," Lieutenant Mulligan told Lieutenant Shapiro. And then he said, "What's going on here anyway? We've got him cold."

"Sounds that way," Nathan Shapiro said.

"Last night," Mulligan said, "the assistant D.A. gave the go-ahead on a homicide charge, and why not, for God's sake? But this morning he calls back and says they're not ready yet and are going to make it material witness. Says that's the way it came to him from the deputy chief of the Homicide Bureau, who's a man named Simmons."

Shapiro said he didn't know anything about that.

"On account of," Mulligan said, "the way we get it it was your boss Weigand, who talked

67

Simmons into holding off for a couple of days anyway. For all we've got Baker cold."

Shapiro didn't know anything about that, either.

"So that's the way it is for now," Mulligan said. "Arraigned as a material witness. I will say for the judge he set bail high enough. Fifty grand, which shows how the judge felt about it, wouldn't you say?"

"Ought to keep Baker," Shapiro said. "The kid got a lawyer?"

"Court-appointed, sure. Made noises about the amount of the bail but the judge didn't hear them. Look, how come Weigand's so interested in an open-and-shut case? Two of your boys sat in last night. They went along with the rest of us."

"The captain," Shapiro said, "wants us to take another look is all."

"Maybe," Mulligan said, "because she wasn't just anybody but this famous actress and it's a hell of a big story. The *Daily News* is off its rocker about it. So's the *Times,* sort of. And the TV boys and everybody. So Weigand wants Homicide to horn in."

"No," Shapiro said. "Weigand doesn't work like that, Lieutenant. Can I see the kid?"

"I said sure, didn't I?" Mulligan said. "With the recorder on."

In some New York City station houses, everything asked and answered in the interrogation room is tape-recorded. Some policemen prefer earlier customs, which allowed more freedom.

"Any way you want it," Shapiro said, and was told, "In there," and went into a small room furnished with a wooden table and wooden chairs and inadequately air-conditioned. He waited for some minutes and a uniformed man opened the door and said "Here he is, Lieutenant." A tall blond boy came into the small room, and the patrolman locked the door behind him.

Roy Baker stood straight just inside the door. He wore his blond hair long. He wore clean, tight denim trousers and a blue polo shirt. He had a wide forehead, and his blue eyes were set far apart. He was a very good-looking boy, in spite of the long hair, Nathan Shapiro thought. And he thought also that Roy Baker had been crying.

"Sit down, Baker," Shapiro said.

"You're another one of them," the boy said, and still stood erect near the door. "I've been telling it over and over the way it was."

"Yes," Shapiro said. "I'm another one of them, son. And I guess we do go over things a good many times. And now I want you to go over it again. They tell you who I am?"

"A lieutenant from the Homicide Squad,"

69

Roy Baker said. "They didn't give me any name."

"Shapiro. You may as well sit down, son."

The tall, handsome boy pulled a chair near the door, so that it was some distance from the chair Nathan Shapiro sat on. The boy sat facing Shapiro. There was no doubt he had been crying. As Shapiro sat and looked at him, the boy's face twitched. But he sat very erect in the straight chair.

"All right, son," Shapiro said. "You worked in this garden of hers yesterday. Until about when, Roy?"

"Until about five, like I told them."

"Yes," Shapiro said, "I know you've been over it all. At about five you'd finished? Or was that your quitting time?"

"Both, man."

"What were you doing?"

Roy Baker said he didn't get it. Then he said he was working.

"Doing what?"

"Weeding. Cultivating. Watering. The things you do in a garden. You know."

Shapiro didn't know, actually. But he nodded his understanding. He said, "Then?"

Then the boy had gone in the back door of the house and found two envelopes, one containing his wages and the other marked "Graduation Gift." He told the rest as he had

70

told it before, speaking without emphasis, using words which, Shapiro realized, had become too familiar for emphasis.

"You didn't use the telephone to call the police," Shapiro said, when the familiar story had been told. "Why was that, Roy?"

"I've read about things like that," the boy said. "You're not supposed to touch anything. On account of fingerprints."

"You knew there wasn't anybody else in the house?"

"Sure. Like it mostly was Sunday afternoons. Maria and Mrs. James are both off Sunday afternoons."

"But you thought Mrs. Singleton might be there. Since you went up, you say, to thank her for the present."

Roy Baker had thought she might be. Mostly she wasn't Sunday afternoons, but sometimes she got home maybe around four.

"She was a good person to work for, Roy?"

"She was all right."

"Friendly to you?"

"Sure. All right, man, she was a swell person to work for. She was a swell person, I guess."

"And," Shapiro said, "apparently a very attractive woman. Did she ever — call it make passes at you, son? Or, say, let you feel you could make passes at her?"

Roy Baker moved as if he were about to

stand up. But he did not stand up. He said, "You're crazy, man. She was old. Maybe she was forty. Old enough to be my mother."

There was no use telling the boy that Jennifer Singleton had been old enough to be his grandmother. For a boy of eighteen, old age may well begin at forty. After that time blurs, grows foggy gray. There was no use telling the boy that sexual interest is not ended by a stop watch marking years. If the boy didn't already know it. There was no use telling the boy that he was a damned good-looking boy to any woman's eyes. That he probably already knew.

"You think I'm a queer or something?" Roy Baker said, unexpectedly.

A good many things people say are unexpected to Nathan Shapiro, who is the first to admit he doesn't understand people very well.

"No," Shapiro said. "It wouldn't have occurred to me, son. I expect you get along all right with girls. They fall for you, don't they, Roy?"

"I get along all right. What's that got to do with anything, man?"

"Nothing, probably," Shapiro said. "You know the layout of the house, Roy? Since you've been working there for — how long was it, son?"

"Since last September," Roy Baker said.

"Sure I know the layout. In the winter I helped out inside. Brought in wood for the fireplaces and helped the cleaning woman with heavy things."

"Did they give you a key to the house? Since, on Sunday afternoons, you'd have to have some way to get in if the cook and the maid — and Mrs. Singleton, of course — were all out."

"Yeah. After I'd been there a few times, the cook gave me a key to the basement door."

"Ever need to use it, Roy?"

"Couple of times, maybe. I'd ring the bell and wait for somebody to let me in. Couple of times nobody came and I used the key."

"Had you been in Mrs. Singleton's bedroom — bedroom suite I guess you'd call it — before yesterday?"

"Sure. Sometimes."

"When Mrs. Singleton was there?"

"Maybe. Sometimes. Mostly when I was helping the cleaning woman, she went out. Said, 'I'll get out from underfoot,' and things like that."

"Never alone in the room with her? With Mrs. Singleton, I mean. In the bedroom, I mean."

"Man, you're crazy."

"Well?"

"Could be. Once or twice. Once she spilled

something on the rug. Cold cream or something, and it was Sunday and she called down
— I was spading up the garden — and had
me go up and take the rug downstairs and
clean it."

"That time," Shapiro said, "how was she
dressed, son?"

"A robe or something, I guess. I just rolled
the rug up and took it down to the basement."

"Was the rug pretty messed up, Roy? Have
trouble getting it cleaned?"

"Not too bad."

"When you went up to get the rug," Shapiro
said. "She'd been doing her face, I suppose.
Spilled the cold cream or whatever it was while
she was doing her face. Have cold cream, or
whatever they use, all over it?"

"I didn't notice."

"Look, son," Shapiro said, and let his voice
harden, "this was a beautiful woman. You're
not a queer. Men look at beautiful women.
This time, whenever it was, you looked at her.
Had she put what they call a 'new face' on?"

Roy hesitated. Perhaps, Shapiro thought,
I've put ideas into his head. Perhaps I haven't
needed to.

"She looked all right," Roy Baker said.
"Way I remember it. For an older woman.
What I keep telling you, she was old enough
to be my mother."

74

"Yes," Shapiro said, "you do keep telling me that, son. By the way, they tell me you live with your father. Your own mother?"

"She's dead, man. When I was a kid she died."

"Sorry," Shapiro said. "Tough not having a mother. You been in trouble before, Roy?"

"Not until now."

"And," Shapiro said, "they tell me you claim you've never owned a switchblade."

"That's the truth, man."

"Ever belong to a gang, Roy?"

"Not the way you mean it. If you mean it bad, and I guess you do. Couple of years ago I went around with some fellows, way everybody does."

"You don't go around, as you put it, with the same fellows any more?"

"No. A lot of them quit school. Anyway —"

He paused. Shapiro waited. Then he said, "Anyway what, son?"

"Some of them wanted to rough up some other guys. I didn't have anything against the other guys. So I said they could count me out."

"They did? Without getting tough about it?"

"Look, man," Roy Baker said. "I can take care of myself."

Shapiro said he was sure of it. He said, "Mrs. Singleton bring friends out to look at her garden, when you were working in it?"

"A few times, maybe."

"Introduce you to any of them?"

"Why would she, man? Oh, couple of weeks ago — a Sunday afternoon, I guess — she brought three or four people out and said, 'Hello, Roy,' and then, when somebody said she'd never seen tulips like those, Mrs. Singleton said, 'It's all Roy's doing, Ruth. He makes things grow.' But that wasn't being introduced. Anyway, all you do with tulips is put the bulbs in the ground and weed around the shoots when they come up."

"That so?" Shapiro said. "You didn't know any of the people she brought out to look at the garden."

"Mr. Gage," Roy said. "He was the one called up the school and said he had a job for a boy who would work at it. When they told me to go over to the house, Mr. Gage was the one I talked to first — Mrs. Singleton too, but mostly Mr. Gage."

"What kind of a man is this Mr. Gage, Roy? You do know he was her husband, don't you?"

"Yes. Only he wasn't around much. What do you mean, what kind of a man?"

"Just that. You liked him?"

"Didn't think about it. Just about getting the job. He did ask a lot of questions, sort of as if he thought I was trying to keep things back. I didn't have anything to keep back, but that was the way it felt."

"But he hired you?"

"Not really. Mrs. Singleton did that herself. Said something like, 'Quit badgering the boy, Joe. And quit being so superior. He'll do.' "

"What does this man Gage look like, Roy?"

"He's good-looking. Dark hair — pretty near black. And taller than I am. Kind of face you remember, sort of. They say he's an actor."

"Younger than Mrs. Singleton was, would you say?"

"Maybe. Not all that young, but it's hard to tell about older people. Maybe in his thirties."

"This woman she called Ruth," Shapiro said. "Use her last name?"

"No."

"Anybody else she called by a first name?"

"Don't remember anybody — yes. There was a man she called 'Les.' Big man with gray hair, only not much of it."

"Seemed friendly with him?"

"They all seemed friendly."

"Two men," Shapiro said. "One of them Mr. Gage and the other this man she called 'Les.' And a woman she called 'Ruth.' That was all came to look at the garden this time you remember?"

"There was another woman came out a little later. After the others, I mean. She had a drink in her hand. They called her 'Joanie,' way I remember it. But I'd got back to work by then."

"That time, or any other time," Shapiro said, "was there a man around they called 'Kurt'?"

Not that Roy Baker could remember.

"She often have people in on Sunday afternoons?"

"Pretty often, I guess."

"Big parties?"

The boy didn't remember any big parties. Except on New Year's Eve, and he'd helped clean up the next day. Mostly, as far as he knew, people would come in Sunday afternoons, but maybe only four or five people.

How did he know that?

Mostly, the small cocktail parties had been in the sitting room of her suite upstairs. He'd be working and now and then would stand up, on account of a man had to stretch, and look up and see people in the sitting room of Mrs. Singleton's suite. In the spring, before the air conditioning was turned on, the windows would be open and he would hear voices. And sometimes people would go out on the balcony and look down at the garden.

"According to what you told them last

night," Shapiro said, "you never owned a switchblade knife."

"That's right."

"Some of the boys at school do?"

"Maybe. Some of the tough ones, maybe."

"At the house," Shapiro said, "you knew where the kitchen knives were kept?"

"Sure."

"But you didn't know that Mrs. Singleton had a drawer — in her desk, I think it was — she put money in for the maid and cook to use for incidental expenses? Things that came up about the house when Mrs. Singleton herself wasn't in it?"

"No. And I know what you're getting at, man. Like I told the others, I didn't know she left money lying around. The money I had on me when this cop grabbed me was my wages and the present she gave me and maybe four-five dollars I had when I went there to work."

The boy stood up suddenly. He moved extremely well and quickly. He walked over and looked down at Nathan Shapiro and his face was working.

"You all think I'm lying," the boy said, and his voice went up. "I can't help what you think, man. The way it was is the way I said it was. When I went in she was lying on the rug and bleeding and I —"

"Yes, Roy," Shapiro said. "You've told us."

"Thing is," the boy said, "none of you listen. All you care about you've got somebody to pin it on. Easy like. Somebody like me with no money to hire a fancy lawyer. The way it always is with the cops."

He tightened his hands into fists and shook them in the air. Then, as suddenly as he had stood up, he sat down in a chair by the wooden table and put his arms on it, and his head down on his arms. And he began to cry.

There was still as much child as man in the boy, Shapiro thought.

"No," he said, "it isn't always that way with the cops, son."

He went over to the door of the small room and knocked on it and a patrolman opened it.

"I've finished with Baker," Shapiro said.

"Just going to tell you the van's here, Lieutenant," the patrolman said. "To pick up Baker."

The van of the Department of Correction would take Roy Baker to the House of Detention for Men. Until somebody posted fifty thousand bond money for him. Which would, Nathan Shapiro thought, be a hell of a long time.

He turned and Baker was standing up. His eyes were red and he dabbed at them with the back of his hands. He didn't look at Shapiro when he walked across the room and out the door. He went down the corridor with the patrolman, not looking at anybody.

"Find out everything you can about the kid." That was what Anthony Cook was supposed to do. From his classmates at Clayton High School; from his teachers there — from everybody who, during the almost four years he had gone to the school, had had contact with Roy Baker. When he started, Cook realized it wasn't going to be easy. After a couple of hours of trying to get answers he had proved it wasn't.

There were too many kids in Clayton High School. There were too many in most of the classes for any one kid to stand out. "Baker?" the teachers said. "There are a good many boys named Baker at the school, Mr. Cook. Could he be a small dark-haired boy? No, the dark one is named Frank, I think. You said Roy?"

"Roy," Cook said, time after time. "A tall blond boy. The one who's now in a little trouble."

A good many of the teachers he talked to didn't know anything about a boy named Roy Baker being in trouble. A few did, and the gym teacher was one of them. He considered

Roy Baker an upstanding young man and a good basketball player, for all he was only six feet tall. He didn't know anything against the kid. Good team spirit the kid had.

"Not been in any trouble you know of?" Cook asked him.

Not that the instructor of physical education had ever heard about. Good athlete. Good enough distance runner and an all-right tennis player. Only trouble was, like with a lot of them, he didn't have time to train properly. Worked after school instead of working *out* after school, if Cook knew what he meant. Didn't give himself a fair chance.

"Some of the kids probably are members of gangs," Cook said. "Know if young Baker was?"

The gym instructor said he didn't. But then he hesitated. He said, "Seems as if, couple of years ago —" and stopped, evidently to consider. After he had he said, "Ever been in trouble with you people?"

"Not that the records show," Cook told him.

"There are some tough guys here," the gym instructor said. "All schools have them. Kids without the team spirit. Learn to spot them in my job."

Cook was sure of it.

"Couple of years ago," the gym instructor

said. "Seems to me I remember the Baker boy was friendly with a few guys who didn't have the team spirit. Not what I'd call the team spirit."

"Gangs?"

"We've got them, I guess. Usually, the kid gangs are mostly dropouts. Some of the boys young Baker seemed to know best have dropped out the last couple of years. Hang around street corners, if you know what I mean. Have fights with other gangs. About territory and that sort of thing. And girls. There are always girls."

Cook told him he had something there. He said, "Recently — last year, say — you think Baker hasn't been seeing so much of these tough kids? What they call delinquent kids?"

"Way I feel about it," the gym instructor said. "But they come through here in droves. Few I get to know a little. Ones on the basketball squad. Track team. Whether, say, they can shoot baskets. And whether they've got the right team spirit. Tell you what, Mr. Cook, whyn't you talk to the staff psychologist?"

Cook said it was a good idea, and acted on it, finding the psychologist with the assistance of Mrs. Rose Shapiro, who said, "Is the boy all right, Mr. Cook?"

"Held as a material witness," Cook told her. "Bail set pretty high. Too high for him to make, which I guess was the idea, Mrs. Shapiro."

"He's a good boy," Rose Shapiro said. "You won't find out he wasn't, Mr. Cook. Is that what you — and my husband, I suppose — are trying to do?"

"Just what kind of a kid he is," Cook said. "This psychologist? Think he'd know?"

"She," Rose told him. "Helen Phipps. Dr. Helen Phipps. Doctorate in psychology. You can try."

Dr. Helen Phipps was a small woman with gray hair in a bun at the back of her head She wore bifocals. She was rather what Cook had supposed she would be. She couldn't place a boy named Roy Baker.

"Which means," she said, "that he hasn't had problems — or been a problem, of course — which would bring him to my attention. However —"

However, there were records. An assistant brought them. Dr. Phipps looked at them. She said, "Hmmm."

"I.Q. one hundred and forty," she said. "Some indication of resentful attitude the first year he was here. According to Dr. Williams, who was an assistant in this department then. Been transferred since. Hmmm. Normal attitude toward sex. Application fair to good. Means to his school work, Mr. Cook. As reported by his teachers. Considered outstanding in English courses by those who have had him in classes. Only fair in mathematics. About all we've got here. As I said, we get the problem ones. The disruptive ones."

"Resentful attitude?"

"Dr. Williams appears to have thought so."

"Sort of attitude which might get him involved with one of these teen-age gangs?"

"It might," she said. "It does, sometimes. They — strike out. Band together and strike out together. But there's nothing on Baker's record."

"His I.Q.? Is one hundred and forty good?"

"Superior. Not genius rating, but superior. What's he supposed to have done, Mr. Cook?"

"He was," Cook told her, "picked up running away from the scene of a crime. Of murder. Of the murder of Mrs. Jennifer Singleton, the actress."

"She was a wonderful actress," Helen Phipps said. "I heard about what happened — about the tragic thing that happened. It is thought young Baker killed her?"

"According to his story," Cook told her, "he found her body. And he was running. He hasn't been charged with homicide. But he's held as a material witness."

"Meaning," Dr. Phipps said, "that you think he killed her, but haven't enough evidence to charge him. It comes to that, doesn't it?"

"Might," Cook said. "Up to the D.A.'s office. I'm just finding out what I can about him."

And he wasn't, he thought, finding out much that was solid. "Resentful" a couple of years ago. Possibly, at about that time, associated with tough kids. Most of whom had dropped out of school. Well, he'd have to try the kids themselves. Which wouldn't be easy. Teen-agers tend to resent cops. They align themselves against cops. Or a lot of them do.

Cook went to talk to kids.

VI

Detectives waste a lot of time. Nathan Shapiro felt that he was wasting his. Not, of course, that his time was of special value to anyone, including the Police Department of the City of New York. Wasting his on a hunch which wasn't even his own hunch — a secondhand hunch, one could call it. He corrected that as he looked in a Manhattan telephone directory under the "G's" for "Gage." Not secondhand. Nothing between him and Rose was secondhand. Her belief in a tall blond boy named Roy Baker wasn't secondhand either. She was seldom wrong about people. Oh, about me, Nathan Shapiro thought. Certainly about me. It is hard to understand, but about me she has a blind spot. Compares me to my father, which is ridiculous. However —

"Gage, Joseph," and a telephone number and an address in the Murray Hill area.

Gage first, if he was to play this hunch, which wasn't his hunch. Gage because he stood to profit from the death of Jennifer

Singleton to the extent of one third of her estate. Unless, of course, she had, in her will or before she wrote a will, got around that. She could have paid him off with the stipulation that the payment was in lieu of dower rights. Ask Gage about that, and about other things.

Only, Shapiro realized after listening for several minutes to a sound that meant a telephone was ringing in an apartment in the Murray Hill area, not ask him right now. Joseph Gage, widower, was not home or not answering his telephone. Conceivably, Joseph Gage, at four o'clock in the afternoon, was out drowning his sorrow. If, of course, he had sorrow which needed drowning. Something to find out about from Gage, when a tall, black-haired actor got home from wherever he was or decided to answer his telephone. Or, of course, his doorbell.

Shapiro flipped the pages of the directory. "Agee, Lester." Probably wouldn't be listed, which would mean a minor wrangle with the New York Telephone Company. Sure enough, "Agee, Lester," and an address in the far east Sixties. Shapiro dialed again and waited again. But this time he waited only briefly and a man said, "Mr. Agee's residence." He said it formally. He believed that Mr. Agee was in. And who wished to speak to Mr. Agee?

88

"Police officer," Shapiro said. "Mr. Agee'll know what about."

His name? Shapiro gave his name and rank. The man said, "One moment, please," and Shapiro said "Sure." He waited rather more than a moment before he heard a different male voice and heard, "Agee." Then Agee said, "About Jenny, I suppose? The damnedest damn thing. Some little squirt kills beauty. Kills —" It trailed off. "God damn it to hell," Lester Agee said. "What do you want of me?"

"To talk to you," Shapiro said.

"You've got the little squirt. The murdering little degenerate. What's there to talk about?"

Shapiro used words to him familiar — words about completing records; words about filling in backgrounds; words about the necessary routine; words about what "they" had told him to do. (The word "they" can cover a multitude of evasions.) He used words about having to go through the formalities.

"You'll be wasting your time," Lester Agee said. "*And* my time."

"Probably. We waste a good deal of it, Mr. Agee. I'll keep it as short as I can, but you're one of the ones I'm supposed to see."

"Why?"

"Because you are one of those who was close to Mrs. Singleton. Can tell us about her."

"That she's dead," Agee said. "You don't

need me to tell you that. That she was a great actress and a great person and some lousy, thieving kid killed her."

"The way it looks," Shapiro said. "In about twenty minutes, Mr. Agee?"

Precinct provided, with no special enthusiasm, a cruise car and a patrolman to drive it. It took a little more than twenty minutes. The apartment house towered in the east Sixties. Shapiro identified himself; the clerk at the desk used his telephone. An elevator carried Shapiro twenty-two floors toward the sky and left him in a carpeted room with two doors opening from it. One door had "Service" lettered on it. The other had numerals, "2201." When Shapiro pressed a button beside the numbered door, chimes sounded softly. Almost at once, a man in a dark suit opened the door. He looked at Nathan Shapiro carefully, and Shapiro realized that his own dark gray suit needed pressing.

"You are Lieutenant Shapiro of the police," the man in the narrow, almost black suit told Shapiro, who said he was.

"Mr. Agee is expecting you," the man told him. "If you will come this way?"

Shapiro went that way behind the man in the narrow suit. He went down a corridor and into an enormous room, with one wall of glass. Beyond the glass, far down, was the East

River. A tug was towing two barges up toward Hell Gate. There was a big empty fireplace in one side wall of the room.

There were four deep green chairs at the end of the room where the wall was glass. In one of them a man was sitting, watching the laboring tugboat. The man in the narrow dark suit cleared his throat and said, "The police lieutenant, Mr. Agee."

The man's chair was on a swivel, and the man swung it to face away from the glass. He was a big man; a heavy man with broad shoulders. A blue polo shirt stretched tight on his bulk, above gray slacks. His feet were bare in the room's deep carpet. Shapiro waded down the room toward him.

"All right," Lester Agee said. "You're here. Sit down." He swiveled his chair so that it faced the one beside it. He flicked a big hand toward that chair and Shapiro went down the room, sinking into the carpet, and sat in the chair.

"The way I get it," Agee said, "you're supposed to show me your badge. That's the way I've seen it staged. And then there's some gobbledygook about everything being taken down and used against me."

The big man's voice rumbled. He had bushy gray eyebrows and gray hair, which was thick only on the sides of his head. "Gray hair and not much of it." That was what a tall blond boy who had too much hair had said.

Shapiro took his badge out of a pocket and held it out toward Lester Agee. Agee did not look at it. He looked at Nathan Shapiro and nodded his head.

"More like it," Agee rumbled. "This sort of thing, you've got to get the business right. The business is damn important. Remember one called *Gaslight?*"

Nathan Shapiro for a moment looked at bright, contorted pictures on the walls of this enormous room. He was over his head again; the pictures reminded him of the last time when he was so obviously and deeply over his head. He said, looking back at the big man, "Gaslight, Mr. Agee?"

"Name of it," Agee said. "Years ago. Scotland Yard inspector or something. Wasn't supposed to be somewhere and left and forgot to take his hat. Left it on a table. Audience damn near went nuts. Some performances, they say, people began to yell, 'Hat. *Hat!*' at the stage. One of the best bits of business anybody ever thought up."

"Oh," Shapiro said, "this was in a play."

"What the hell," Agee said, "did you think it was in?"

"You'd lost me," Shapiro said. "I don't know much about the theater, Mr. Agee."

"Television, probably," Agee said. "Or movies. It's people like you are letting the theater starve. You know that, Lieutenant?"

"It costs a lot to go to the theater," Shapiro said, wondering how far adrift a man could get. "Did this inspector go back and get his hat, Mr. Agee?"

"Yes," Agee said. "Just when the audience was ready to fall apart. Swell business. Swell timing. You didn't come here to talk about the theater, did you?"

"No," Shapiro said. "About Mrs. Singleton."

"Then," Agee said, "get on with it, man. What about Jenny? Except that she was a beautiful person and a damned good actress. I don't say great. No, I don't say great. But most of the time it was hard to tell the difference. Except in comedy. I'll give you that. But with that laugh of hers it didn't matter if her comedy timing was a little off sometimes. And a no-count little rat kills her. *Kills* her, damn it. Kills *Jenny*."

Agee closed his eyes then and moved his heavy head from side to side and then, suddenly, he began to pound on the arm of his chair with his right hand. He pounded the padded arm in rhythm, as if to count in his mind. Shapiro sat and looked at him. Agee stopped beating the arm of the chair and sat quiet with his eyes still closed. Then, abruptly, he got out of the deep chair and walked across the room to a bar. Standing, he was an even bigger man, and a harder one. He walked with quick assurance.

He made himself a drink and, holding it, turned to face Shapiro. He said, "O.K. Why don't you get on with it?" He stood with his back to the bar and waited.

"Yesterday evening," Shapiro said, "you went to Mrs. Singleton's house. Why?"

"To take her to dinner."

"And?"

"And found the street full of police cars," Agee said, and took a long swallow from his glass. "And cops all around the place. And men in civilian clothes — I suppose they were cops too? — going in and out of the house. I started to go in and a patrolman stopped me and I asked what the hell gave and he told me. Told me Jenny'd been killed."

He put the glass down hard on the bar — hard enough, almost, to break it. It didn't break.

"Then?"

"Somebody — a man in civilian clothes — asked me who I was and I told him and then — it's a little dim. Jumbled up in my mind. Then, I guess, I just walked away and got a cab. I remember — think I remember —

words going over and over in my mind. '*She's dead. Jenny's dead. Jenny's dead.*' Trying to take it in. What difference does it make? The way I felt, I mean."

"I don't know," Shapiro said. "I don't, right now, know what makes a difference. It hit you hard, her death? But obviously it hit you hard."

"Any of your business, Lieutenant?"

"Anything I can find out about her is my business," Shapiro said. "You had an engagement with her for last evening?"

"I was taking her to dinner."

"You saw a good deal of her? In spite of being divorced from her? In spite of the fact that she was married to another man?"

"I saw a good deal of her. This other man — that was over. Washed up. A twerp, Gage is. Sometimes she fell for twerps. Got over them. What's it to you?"

Again, Shapiro didn't know.

"Nothing to do with this young hoodlum killing her."

"No," Shapiro said. "If he did kill her."

"Then why the hell can't you leave her alone? Leave me alone? You people've got this damned kid who killed her."

"We've got a kid," Shapiro said. "Says he didn't kill her. If he didn't, somebody else did. So, we've got to look into all the chances."

Agee walked back to his chair. But now he leaned forward in it and looked at Shapiro.

"Mean something special by that?" he said, and his voice rumbled the words. "Like, did I kill her? When she was the only thing in the whole damned world that mattered a damn? Is that what you're working around to?"

"Just working around," Shapiro said. "The way they tell me to, Mr. Agee. You still loved her, Mr. Agee?"

"We were going to get married again, as soon as she got rid of the Gage twerp."

"Divorce him? She'd started proceedings?"

"Yes. Finally realized there was no point in going on the way they were going on. Married and not married."

"You have anything to do with her coming to this decision?"

"It's none of your damn —" Agee said, but Shapiro leaned forward in his own chair. He cut in on Agee's rumbling words. He said, "Listen, Mr. Agee," and, to his surprise, Agee let his sentence hang and said, "O.K. To what?"

"You loved Mrs. Singleton, you say," Shapiro said. "If the kid we've got didn't kill her, you must want, as much as we want, to find out who did. So, it's your business too, isn't it? Did Gage know she was planning to divorce him? That you and she were going to re-marry?"

"She'd told him. She — she wasn't the sort who did things under cover. Hid them. You didn't know her."

"No," Shapiro said. "You did, apparently. Knew her very well."

"For a lot of years."

"And wrote a good many plays with her in mind? As a star in them?"

"Yes."

"And for Kurt Morton to star in with her?"

"What everybody knows," Agee said.

"She left Morton and married you. Then left you and married Gage. But you and she kept on seeing each other. Being friends. Again, did you persuade her to start divorce proceedings against Gage?"

"We talked it over. But she went her own way about it. She always went her own way about things. You really think the kid didn't kill her?"

"It's possible he didn't."

"Then ask Joe Gage where he was last evening about — when about?"

"Five," Shapiro told him. "Why Gage?"

"She had a lot of money," Agee said. "Still married to her, Gage would get a wad of it, wouldn't he?"

"Probably. On the subject of money, Mr.

Agee. Was she getting a share of your royalties from this play she was in? This last play of hers? And yours, of course?"

"Now what the hell," Agee said, "makes you think that?"

"A man named Temple told the man I'm working with that that might be the setup."

"Temp," Agee said, "is a nosy bastard. Always was. None of his business what I do with my own money, is it?"

Shapiro said he shouldn't think so.

"And none of yours," Agee said.

"Probably not. Was Mrs. Singleton cut in on your royalties from the play?"

"Yes. We'd arranged it that way. My idea, not hers."

"Not a usual arrangement, is it? I wouldn't know."

"I wouldn't either. Not with me it isn't. Hadn't been before."

"Your idea, you say. Mind telling me why? Without telling me it's none of my business? Because, Mr. Agee, I'm not trying to do any pushing around."

"Just nibbling around," Agee said. "Nibbling here and nibbling there. What it comes to, isn't it?"

Shapiro decided that question didn't need an answer.

"All right," Agee said. "The idea for *Always*

Good-bye was partly hers. She had a lot of ideas for plays for her to star in. Talked to me about them. Even wrote down scenes. No good at that. Damn good at knowing what would be right for her. Have a part she'd be good in. Mostly, her ideas weren't plays at all. Just roles for Jennifer Singleton."

"This one was different?"

This one had been. She had had an idea in this one when she told it to Lester Agee. It wasn't, Agee told Lieutenant Nathan Shapiro, any idea that was going to shake the world. It was a situation, more than an idea — the situation a professional woman found herself in when she gave up her profession to marry a man who had never had one but was very rich. "How she adjusted, or tried to," Agee said. "Obviously based on her own experience when she was married to Singleton. You know about that?"

"Yes."

"You've seen *Always Good-bye?*"

"No, Mr. Agee. I told you I don't go to the theater much."

"More or less what it's about," Agee said. "Oh, not the way she first worked it out. All serious as hell, the way she told it to me, a little bit at a time and sometimes a lot at a time. Full of implications. Surprised me, on the whole. Well as I knew her. Some of it didn't sound like her."

"But your play was based — partly, anyway — on her ideas? Which was why you cut her in on the royalties?"

"I used bits and pieces," Agee said. "Turned it into comedy. Yes, I did cut her in. No formal arrangement — no collaborator's contract, or anything like that. Just an understanding between friends."

"You say she'd had ideas for plays before. Told you about them. Did you ever cut her in before?"

"I told you this was different. Her other ideas — hell, you couldn't call them ideas. Just parts for her to star in. Nothing I could use, or did use."

"You saw a good deal of her, I gather," Shapiro said. "At her house, usually?"

"Picked her up there and took her places. After she threw young Gage out. Now and then she'd have people in for drinks and I'd be one of them. Sometimes I'd have people here for drinks and she'd come. And we'd go to parties together. Mostly on Sundays, of course. When she wasn't working."

"I've got to ask a lot of things," Shapiro said. "Matters of routine. Things for the record. Do you have a key to her house, Mr. Agee? Or, did you ever have?"

"Did I let myself in yesterday? Wait in her

upstairs living room — what she called her 'quarter' — and kill her when she came in? That's what you're really asking, isn't it?"

"Whether you had a key to the house," Shapiro said. He let weariness sound in his voice.

"No. I didn't. Oh, when we were married. Sure. And when she said she'd found the man she really loved — meaning this twerp Gage — and went off to Reno, I gave her back the key. Played it as a scene, she did, and I played along. She played most things as scenes. Which didn't mean that, to her, the things weren't real. It was her idiom to play her life in scenes."

"You didn't have a key to her house. When you went there to see her you rang the doorbell and somebody let you in?"

"Like anybody else. Sure."

"Happen to know whether Gage had a key to the house?"

Agee said he didn't. He said that, at a guess, Jenny would have played a scene with Gage when she threw him out. The "give-me-back-my-doorkey" scene. He said that that was only a guess. He said, "It's easy enough to have a key copied, Lieutenant."

"By anyone," Shapiro said. "When did she throw Gage out, as you put it?"

"Last fall."

"And had been married to him how long?"

"Couple of years. Six months or so after our divorce became final she married the twerp."

"You called him 'young' Gage," Shapiro said. "A good deal younger than she was?"

"Put it one way," Agee said, "nobody was younger than Jenny. But the way you mean it, a hell of a lot younger. She was — oh, damn near sixty. Probably you've looked that up."

"Yes," Shapiro said. "And Gage?"

"In his thirties somewhere," Agee said. "I never asked him. At a guess, in his thirties. And, before you nibble at it, I'm pretty close to ten years younger than she was. And Kurt Morton is about my age. And what does that get you?"

"Nothing, probably."

"That she robbed cradles? Went after younger men? That —" He broke off suddenly. Then he said, "This kid you've got. Good-looking kid?"

"I'd call him that."

"No," Agee said. "You're getting her all wrong. She wasn't like that. Oh, she noticed when a man was good-looking. What woman doesn't? As men notice good-looking women. But what you're implying — you're getting her all wrong. Applying the wrong standards. All right, policemen's standards."

"Well," Shapiro said, "I'm a policeman. We run into all sorts. And try to sort them out. I'm not implying anything about Mrs. Singleton. Just trying to find out about her."

"This kid you've got. Does he imply anything? Boast about anything? Because if he does, he's a damn liar."

"He doesn't," Shapiro said. "I gave him a chance to. Not, of course, that it would have been a chance he'd have wanted to take."

"All right," Agee said. "We circle around it, don't we? Did this kid rape her? Or try to? There'd be ways of knowing if he had, wouldn't there? I mean —"

Then he closed his eyes as he had before and, as before, rhythmically pounded the padded arm of his chair. Again, Shapiro waited. After a time, Agee rested his arm on the chair arm and opened his eyes.

"They did an autopsy? Cut —" His heavy face worked and for a moment he did not go on. He swallowed, as if he tried to swallow words. Or thoughts. "Cut her up," he said.

"Yes," Shapiro said. "It's always done. To make certain of the cause of death. Among other things. No, Mr. Agee. She hadn't been raped. Just stabbed. Once. She must, they say, have lost consciousness almost immediately. Have died within a minute or two."

"Something," Agee said. "Not much, but

something. Not — not hurt before he killed her? Or, somebody killed her?"

"No."

"Did you see her. Her — her body? Go and stare at her?"

"No. Oh, others did. Had to. And took pictures. Had to do that, too."

"You, yourself, never saw her."

"Only her picture," Shapiro said. "She was beautiful."

"Then," Agee said, "you never heard her laugh. *Never heard her laugh.*"

"No," Shapiro said. "She had a special kind of laughter?"

"I can't describe it," Agee said. "Nobody could ever describe it. Reviewers, people like that, tried for years to find words to — oh, to describe magic. Nobody ever did. They said things like 'low' and 'rippling' and 'infectious.' Said all the usual things. And, of course, that it was 'unique.' A handy word to say nothing with. Do you read poetry, Lieutenant?"

"Sometimes," Shapiro said. "Not much."

"Some poetry," Agee said, "does odd things to people. To some people. Almost physical things. There's a kind of stirring all through you when you read some poetry. A kind of exaltation. A feeling of utter rightness. That — hell, I can't find the words for it. That never happened to you?"

"With music sometimes. Not with words."

"Jenny's laughter did that — something like that — to people. Sang in them. Made them, when they heard it, different people — gayer people. For the moment. While she laughed. But I told you, didn't I, that there's no way to describe her laughing. Her speaking voice too. But it was when she laughed —"

He stopped talking and closed his eyes again for a moment. "All right," he said then, "this doesn't get you anywhere, does it?"

"Anything which will tell us about her," Shapiro said. "I don't know what gets us anywhere. We feel our way. Ask the questions we have to ask. Get the facts, or what we're told are the facts. Find out, as well as we can, who people are. And, of course, where they were."

"So," Agee said, "you're getting to that. I was here. Working. And alone in the apartment. And Mimms was out, probably at a movie. He usually is Sunday afternoon."

"Mimms?" It sounded improbable.

"The man who takes care of me," Agee said. "The man who let you in."

"Sunday," Shapiro said. "You work on Sundays, Mr. Agee?"

Lester Agee looked entirely surprised. He looked at Nathan Shapiro as if Shapiro had

105

asked an incredible question. When he spoke, he spoke slowly, as if he doubted whether Shapiro was familiar with English.

"I," Agee said, "am a professional writer. I write for a living. Sunday is like any other day. Sunday and the Fourth of July and Christmas. When I'm onto something, or am trying to get onto something. Do policemen take Sundays off, Lieutenant? Convenient for criminals, that would be."

"No," Shapiro said. "Sunday is like any other day, Mr. Agee. Speaking of writing. Do you know a man named Pierson? Clarke Pierson. He says he knows you. Or, anyway, has met you."

"Pierson?" Agee said. "Can't say I do." He narrowed his eyes and, after a moment, shook his head. "Can't say I do," he said. "Who's he?"

"A man who thinks highly of the kid we've got in jail," Shapiro said. "Thinks he's a brilliant kid. And that the kid is, if he gets out of this, going to be a writer."

"God help him," Agee said. "The kid, I mean. Pierson?"

"He teaches something called 'creative writing' at the high school young Baker goes to," Shapiro said. "And wrote a play once that you —"

"*That* Pierson," Agee said. "Kind of a wispy little guy?"

"He could be called that."

"Wrote a wispy little play a few years ago," Agee said. "Played what amounted to a one-night stand, as I remember it. Yes, he was around for a while and I guess I ran into him. So that's what he's doing now. 'Creative writing,' for the love of God. And this kid wants to be a writer?"

"Apparently."

"Then there's a kid," Agee said, "who's *really* in trouble."

VII

Talking to the other kids at Clayton High School hadn't, Detective Anthony Cook decided after a couple of hours of trying it, got him much of anywhere. For one thing, and perhaps the chief thing, the kids didn't want to talk to cops. For the most part, the kids were evasive with cops; didn't, obviously, want to get mixed up with cops, even to the extent of telling a cop what they knew about another kid.

He stopped kids at random in the school's wide corridors as they went from class to class. There were hundreds of kids; his sampling was, of necessity, hit-and-miss. "Yeah," a kid said, "think I know him. All-right guy, far's I know." Which didn't help particularly. "Stuck up," a girl said. "Think's he's God's gift to something. Because he's attractive, maybe." "Yeah," a tall Negro boy said, "I know him, man. He's a square, man."

"Just seen him around," another boy said. "Way I get it, he didn't join in much. Know what I mean?"

"Join in what?" Cook asked that one.

"Things," the boy said. "Like making a pitch about the lousy mess you guys have got us into."

Cook didn't get this one, and said so. Did the boy mean the police had got them into a lousy mess?

"Like everybody else," the boy said. "Worse, maybe. Because it's guys like you push us around when we got rights."

That didn't make it much clearer to Cook. He made a guess. "Antiwar demonstrations?" was his guess.

The boy said, "Sure. Part of it. Show people where our generation stands. On a lot of things, mister. Take me. Soon as I'm old enough to get a draft card, I'm going to burn it. So you want to arrest me?"

That one was one of the more articulate. A good many, among those who said anything, used words which, apparently, had a special meaning. It was, to Cook, as if they spoke in code.

One he stopped in the corridor — a boy with slanting, Oriental eyes — used English with greater care. "I know him to say hello to," this boy said. "I'm in an English class with him. He is a very earnest student, sir. A conformist, if you understand me. What is sometimes called a square."

When he had a chance to make a choice among the kids he asked about Roy Baker, Cook chose males and, after an hour or so of getting nothing much, those who looked, to the experienced eyes of a policeman, like tough kids. They were among the least talkative. But when they talked at all, they seemed to know less than the others about Roy Baker. They might, of course, be covering for him. But it was not clear what, if anything, they were covering — except, of course, themselves. Had Roy been a member of a gang? "Don't know what you're talking about, man. No gangs in this school I know of."

Cook found a girl — a pretty girl — who was in Mr. Pierson's creative writing class with Roy Baker. "We write things," she explained. "Mr. Pierson reads some of them aloud for group criticism. Stories and things like that."

"Any of Roy's?"

"A couple, anyway. Pretty grim things, both of them were. Like there was no hope in anything. Only Mr. Pierson seemed to think they were good."

"You didn't?"

"Like my father says, there're enough sordid things without having to read about them."

"Sordid? Roy's stories were sordid?"

"About people without any money, living in slums," the girl said.

"He's a good-looking boy," Cook said. "How did most of the girls feel about him?"

"All right, I guess. Not me, if that's what you're getting at."

"At general impressions," Cook said.

"Right after school," the girl said, "Roy was always rushing off somewhere. Too busy to stand around and talk, the way most of us do. Or go somewhere for a Coke. Like he had a job to do or something."

That did recur — Roy Baker had not mixed much with the other students. If he had made friends, the boys and girls Cook could persuade to talk had not been among them. Cook was left the impression from his random sampling that Roy Baker had merely gone, almost anonymously, to Clayton High School; that he had not really been a part of it. And that proved nothing about Roy Baker. The kid had had part-time jobs to do for the money in them. Probably it was as simple as that. He had had little time to be a kid among other kids at Clayton High School. Which, of course, he might have resented.

"Like there was no hope in anything," the girl had said of stories by Roy Baker a teacher had read aloud to the class. Stories "about people without any money, living in slums."

Cook looked at his watch. It was a little after five. He walked down Sixth Avenue to Morton Street. On one side of the block he walked through were solid houses in a row. On the other side were old-law tenements, with fire escapes zigzagging up them. In the entrance hall of the one of the tenements which had the right street address slips of paper in slots listed names. After the name "Ralph Baker" on one of the slips there was further direction. "4R" was printed after Baker's name. "Four rear," Cook decided, and climbed a narrow staircase which leaned uncertainly against the wall.

A square of paper — yellowed paper — was thumbtacked to one of the doors on the fourth floor. It had "Baker" printed on it. Cook knocked on the door. When there was no answer he knocked again. There was still no answer, but he heard below him the creaking of stairs as somebody walked up them. Whoever it was walked to the third floor and along the hallway and came on up.

Cook looked down at a tall, light-haired man who had his suit coat slung over his shoulder. A few steps from the landing the man stopped and looked up at Cook. He said, "Looking for somebody, mister?"

There was an unshaded light bulb glowing dimly in an outlet set into the ceiling of the fourth-floor hallway. It dripped light on the top of the man's head and made shadows of cheekbones down his face.

"For Ralph Baker," Cook said. "Happen to be you?"

"Sure as hell does," the man said. "And if you're the one after the rent again —"

"No," Cook said. "Just like a word with you, Mr. Baker. About your son. I'm a police detective."

"You've got the kid wrong," Baker said. "He's a good kid. Whatcha want me to tell you about him?"

He came on up and Cook stepped aside to let him reach the door. He stopped in front of it.

"Think I'm gonna help you frame my own kid?" Baker said.

"Nothing like that," Cook told him. "And nobody's trying to frame your son, Mr. Baker."

"Hell," Baker said, "I know cops. Got a warrant, or something?"

"No warrant," Cook said. "Just trying to find out what we can about the kid. What they call background. Thing we always have to do, cases like this."

Baker fished a key out of his pocket and opened the door. He went through it and left it open and Cook went through it after him.

He went into a small room with a narrow, and unmade, bed against one wall and a table with two chairs drawn up to it in the middle of the room. There was a hard-looking upholstered chair against the wall opposite the bed. At the rear of the room there was an open door and beyond it another room. The back room had a window in it. The window was unexpectedly clean. Through it, Cook could look across an open space and at another tenement.

Baker, without saying anything, went into the back room and to his right, turning out of sight. Cook waited, standing with his back to the entrance door. He heard a refrigerator door opened and then a drawer opened and a clunking sound. Baker came back into the front room with a punctured can of beer. He sat on the unmade bed and tilted his head back to pour beer into his mouth.

There was something vaguely familiar about this tall man, who probably was in his forties and certainly needed a shave. He looked, Cook thought, a little as his son might look in twenty-five years or so. Perhaps that, Cook thought, is the reason I feel I've seen this man before. It's because he looks like the mug shot of the kid.

When Baker raised his head to drink his beer Cook saw a thin scar under his chin.

Then Cook remembered.

"Been about ten years, hasn't it?" Cook said. "Maybe eleven."

Baker merely looked at him over the beer can. Then he shook his head. He said, "What's been ten years, mister?"

"Since you went after a man in a saloon uptown," Cook said. "Only they called it a cocktail lounge."

"Don't know what you're talking about. What you think you're talking about."

"Help you remember," Cook said and pulled one of the chairs away from the table and sat on it, straddling. "I was one of the cops who broke it up. In uniform then. In a patrol car with a sergeant, and we got the signal. Fight in a bar on West — West what street, Baker?"

"Nope," Baker said. "Like the kids say, I don't dig you."

"Sixty-fourth," Cook said. "Maybe Sixty-fifth. Pretty well over toward the river. From what we got, you walked in, all hostile, and there was this man sitting in a booth with a woman. You yanked him out and knocked him down. That's the way we got it. Just like that. And he hit you a couple of times and you knocked him down again. And this broad who'd been with him started yelling and — maybe I oughtn't to call her a broad, Baker.

Seeing she was your wife. Name of — what was her name, Baker? Long time ago, it was."

"Somebody else you're thinking of," Ralph Baker said and tilted the can up to his lips again. "Somebody looked like me, maybe."

"Somebody," Cook said, "with a scar like that one you've got. Somebody used a knife on you once, didn't they? And, from where he got you, you were pretty lucky to stay alive."

"When I was a kid," Baker said. "Window glass. Some kid heaved a rock and I was sitting inside. Only time anybody pulled a knife on me was when Jim —" And with that he stopped and put his can down hard on a table by the bed. The can made an empty clang when he put it down.

"James Brady," Cook said. "That was the man you beat up that night. Comes back to me now. And the woman — your wife, I mean — was named Myra. And Brady says it was you who pulled the knife. After you used your fists. When he got up and came at you the second time. That's when he says you pulled a knife on him."

"He always was a lying bastard," Baker said. "A bastard son of a bitch. I never owned a knife. He pulled it and I took it away from him. Like I told the judge. And like two three guys who saw what happened told the judge.

116

And the judge went along. Or didn't you know that?"

"Suspended sentence," Cook said. "On an assault charge. Not aggravated, because the judge didn't have enough evidence to show him whose knife it was. And whosever it was, you hadn't used it. It keeps coming back to me, Baker."

"Got nothing to do with anything about the kid," Baker said. "So, ten years ago, I roughed up a bastard my wife was two-timing me with. He had it coming, and maybe that's what the judge thought. I was a hell of a lot younger then and I got mad easy."

"What ever became of Myra?" Cook asked him, and Baker said, "How the hell do I know? Went off and shacked up with Brady, like she'd been doing all along. And who she shacked up with after that I don't know, and don't give a damn."

"Roy thinks his mother is dead," Cook said. "Myra was his mother?"

"Sure she was his mother. He tell you she was dead?"

"Not me," Cook said. "Lieutenant I work with."

"Could be," Baker said, "that's the way he wants to think it was. Instead of that she was a no-good bitch."

"You and he have lived together since his mother took off?"

"He was a little kid then," Baker said. "For a while my mother took care of him. About twelve he was when she died. Since then the kid and I've been together."

"Here?"

"Other places too. Here for three-four years."

"What do you work at, Baker?"

Baker stood up and walked again into the rear room. From that room he called, "Want a beer?"

Cook said he didn't want a beer, and Baker came back with another punctured can and sat where he had sat before. He drank. He said, "What's it got to do with the kid what I do for a living?"

"Nothing, probably," Cook said. "Any secret about it?"

"Clerk in a grocery store up the street," Baker said. "No law against that, is there?"

"No," Cook said. "Why'd there be a law against that?"

"What I said," Baker said, and swallowed beer.

"Worked there long?"

"Six months, maybe."

"Before that?"

"Other places. A while I was a janitor — what they call a superintendent. Gave the kid and me a place to live, that did. So what the hell has this got to do with the kid?"

The question was evidently reasonable. Cook wished an answer were.

"Just trying to get Roy's background," Cook said. "Sort of thing we have to try to fill in."

"Done what I could for the kid after she walked out on us," Baker said. "Kept him in school, since he was so goddamn set on it. On what I've been making, that wasn't easy, mister."

"He helped keep himself in school," Cook said. "Finding jobs. Like this one he had with Mrs. Singleton. You ever run into Mrs. Singleton, Baker?"

"Why the hell should I? You think she came into this place I work and picked up her own groceries? This cook of hers did that."

"Oh," Cook said, "she did trade at this place you work? So of course you knew who she was when Roy went to work there."

"Listen," Baker said, "everybody in this part of the Village knew about her. Knew who she was."

"When the cook bought things at the store," Cook said. "She carry them home? Or did somebody deliver them?"

"If she ordered a lot of stuff," Baker said, "it got sent over."

"You ever deliver things to her? Yourself, I mean."

"Couple of boys do that," Baker said. "Mostly, anyway."

"You never did yourself?"

"Maybe a couple of times. When one of the kids was off. Wasn't supposed to be my job, but sometimes we get jammed up."

"When you did deliver to her house, you ever see Mrs. Singleton? Because, with your boy working there, you'd naturally be interested in the place he was working and the kind of woman he was working for."

"Listen," Baker said. "Couple of times I delivered to her, they let me in through the basement and I carried whatever it was to the back yard and then up to the kitchen. How'd I meet Mrs. Singleton? I used the back door. Like I was told."

"Sure," Cook said. "It figures. By the way, Mrs. Singleton charge things at the store?"

"Paid cash the times I delivered," Baker said. "This cook would tell me to wait and she'd go somewhere — upstairs, I guess — and come back with the money. One time, I remember, she came back with a fifty-dollar bill and asked me could I change it. I sure as hell couldn't."

"And?"

"And what?"

"You didn't get paid?"

"Sure I got paid. The cook got her handbag

120

and paid me out of that."

"Say anything?"

"To herself, way I remember it. Sort of grumbling. About 'she' ought to know better than to leave fifties in that drawer of hers. Something like that."

"Drawer of hers?"

"Listen, mister," Baker said. "Maybe I didn't go to school much, but I can read. In the paper, it said the police theory was my kid was taking money out of a drawer she kept it in and she walked in on him and so he stabbed her. Which is one damned lie."

"No," Cook said. "Just the way it looks, Baker. Maybe it wasn't the way it looks. What we're trying to find out."

"Like hell you are. My kid comes handy, so you pin it on my kid."

There was no use telling him the Homicide Squad didn't work that way. Cook told him anyway. He got the short, four-letter answer he expected.

"Roy ever mention to you that Mrs. Singleton kept household money in a drawer in her room?"

"No."

"You ever tell him about this time the cook came back with a fifty you couldn't change?"

"Not that I remember offhand. Maybe I did; maybe I didn't."

"Sometimes," Cook said, "when a kid has a more or less regular job in a house, like Roy had at Mrs. Singleton's house, they give him a key. So that he can get in and work when there's nobody home. A kid they trust."

Baker wouldn't know about that.

"Whether Roy had a key or not?"

"Never said anything about having a key."

"You'd think he would, sort of," Cook said. "Be pleased they trusted him that much."

"Didn't."

"You and the kid got along all right? Talked things over?"

"Sure. Except when he's here, and's got his chores done, he mostly goes into the other room and studies. And sometimes I go out for a beer."

"Sure," Cook said. "Yesterday afternoon — round five maybe — were you out for a beer, Baker? Maybe at a bar where some of the guys know you?"

"You trying to lay it on me? First the kid and then me? That the way it is?"

"No. Just asking questions. No reason you shouldn't be having a beer with some guys you know. In a cool bar somewhere. Must have been hot here yesterday."

"Yesterday," Baker said, "I went to a ball game. And the Mets lost!"

"Yes," Cook said. "I know they lost. Roy

helps you keep this place cleaned up. That's what you meant by chores?"

"Sure he does. He's a good kid. Sort of old-maidish about keeping the place cleaned up. Takes after his mother, could be. She was a bitch most ways, but she kept house."

"She have a job when you and she were living together?"

"Yeah. She was a waitress. Way she met this Brady son of a bitch. And maybe others I didn't find out about. So what's that got to do with your trying to frame the kid?"

He did not wait for an answer. He got up from the bed the kid hadn't been around to make that morning and went into the other room for another beer.

Cook didn't wait for him to come back. Cook had, he decided, got the picture, for what it was worth. Cook went down tilting stairs and got a subway uptown.

An emotional man, Nathan Shapiro thought of Lester Agee. He went down in the elevator from Agee's big apartment and walked a gritty sidewalk in afternoon heat with the sun in his face. Emotional and shaken up by what had happened, Agee was. Odd he hadn't, when he had gone to the house of the woman he was in love with and been told she had been murdered, done more than merely walk away.

Only perhaps it wasn't really odd. There would have been nothing he could do to alter tragic finality. It had been rational merely to walk away. Walk away in shock, perhaps, rather than in reason.

Agee was a man hard hit, Shapiro thought. Or, of course, a good actor. In the theater, Agee was. Had he ever acted in it? He had written with actors in mind; must, Shapiro supposed, have known enough about acting — about what was possible and what was not — to write with actors in mind. Something I don't know anything about, Shapiro thought. A whole kind of life I don't know anything about. I'm no good at understanding people like Agee or, come to that, like Jennifer Singleton. I'm groping around in a world I don't know anything about. Like always.

He walked toward a bus stop. Near it, he found a sidewalk telephone booth and, again, dialed Joseph Gage's number. Again, Gage didn't answer. Shapiro waited for a bus and finally was trundled slowly across town. He went the rest of the way to West Twentieth Street by subway, which was quicker, if somewhat harder to breathe in.

Write a summary, in official terms, of a day's wasted time. Check with Cook when Cook came back from talking with teachers and with kids at Clayton High School. See whether Cook's informants in a world about which, apparently, Cook knew something had told him that Lester Agee, at present a playwright, had ever been an actor. Tell Bill Weigand that he'd found nothing which especially reinforced a borrowed hunch; that it still looked like being the kid. Call it a day and go home to Brooklyn and to Rose and tell her that it still looked like being the kid. She wouldn't like that.

No reason that Gage should be home merely because the police wanted to talk to him. Be interesting, of course, to find out whether Gage knew that, after divorcing him, Jennifer Singleton had planned to remarry Agee. Be interesting, also, to find out if he still had a key to the "mansion" on Point Street. And where he had been the afternoon before. If the motive for murder wasn't merely that a kid had been walked in on while he was stealing a hundred dollars or so, it might conceivably be that Gage didn't want to lose God knew how much more, as he might if a divorce went through. Be interesting to know details of Jennifer Singleton's will. Precinct was working on that, of course. It was still precinct's case. Only, precinct figured it was a solved case. Precinct might reasonably be perfunctory about side issues.

Too late in the day now to catch Mrs.

Singleton's lawyer at his office. Assuming anybody had bothered to find out —

Shapiro shuffled reports on his desk. Nobody had come up with bail money for Roy Baker. The Medical Examiner's autopsy showed that Jennifer Singleton had been white, female and well nourished. She had been in good health until a knife had severed the aorta near her heart. Mrs. Singleton's lawyers, who had been duly notified of what radio and television and newspapers had already told them, were Barclay, Stapleton and Wolfe. They had offices in East Thirty-ninth Street.

Shapiro looked up a telephone number and dialed it, although it was almost six o'clock in the afternoon. He got, as he had supposed he would, an answering service, which said, sweetly, that it was Barclay, Stapleton and Wolfe and that if any associate of the firm called in he would be told that Lieutenant — what was that again? — Lieutenant Shapiro of the New York Police had called.

It was taking Tony Cook longer than Shapiro had supposed it would. The afternoon session at Clayton High School must have been over long ago, and the pupils and their teachers long since scattered beyond the reach of inquiry. Possibly Cook had come on something and was chasing it down. Wait, obviously, until Cook came in, or called in. Have

126

another go at Joseph Gage, although that probably was not much more than a way of twiddling thumbs to occupy time. He dialed Gage's number, which was becoming a familiar one. He waited half a dozen rings for an answer he didn't get. He dialed a number far more familiar. The voice which answered brightened the late fragment of a wasted day.

"Looks," Nathan Shapiro told Rose, "as if I'll be late."

"The way it always looks, darling," Rose said. "Next time I'll marry a nine-to-fiver. About the boy?"

"Nothing to prove anything one way or another," Shapiro told his wife. "We're talking to people."

"He's a good boy," Rose said. "Come home when you can, dear. There's pastrami."

Cook came into the squad room. He looked hot and a little tired. He pulled a chair up to Shapiro's desk.

"Nothing at the school that gets us anywhere," Cook said. "Or that I can see gets us anywhere. There are a hell of a lot of kids there. Our kid doesn't seem to have made much of an impression on the other kids."

"Not on the girls?" Shapiro asked him. "Good-looking kid like he is?"

If Roy Baker had made an impression on the girls, Cook said, he himself hadn't asked the right girls. "Take a week to really get any-where," Cook said. "A week and a half a dozen of us. And the kids are cop-shy. The ones I talked to —"

Cook told, briefly, of his interviews with students and teachers at Clayton High School.

"After school," Shapiro said, "he seems to have worked. For Mrs. Singleton. Maybe at other jobs. Limit his social life."

"Seems to have," Cook said. "After the kids, and most of the teachers, left for the day, I went around to see the kid's father. He —"

Cook told Shapiro about the kid's father.

"Well," Shapiro said. "Might account for the kid's ways. Reaction against a father who hadn't got much of anywhere. Including very far in school. He said that?"

"Yes."

"And who beat up a man his wife was two-timing him with. And who maybe pulled a knife."

"He says not," Cook said. "We couldn't find anybody — except this guy Brady — who'd say Baker pulled a knife. And nobody got cut."

"Roy would have been seven or eight," Shapiro said. "Old enough to know that his mother cleared out. That she didn't die. But he said she was dead. Covering up, at a guess. Hurt and covering up the hurt. Baker says he didn't know his son had a key to the Singleton house. But did know that there was money loose in a drawer somewhere. Money the cook could get to pay for groceries."

Repeating things is a way of fixing them in the mind. It is Nathan Shapiro's belief that a lot of things slip out of his mind unless he pins them there.

"He could have known about the key," Cook said. "Could have got hold of it and had it copied. Could have found out from the kid that the servants, and Mrs. Singleton herself, were likely to be out on Sunday afternoons."

"And," Shapiro said, "got his own kid in a jam. In a way framed his own kid. Sort of man who would, you think, Tony?"

"I don't know I'd put it past him," Cook said. "Lots of people go out to see the Mets get walloped. No way of telling whether our friend Baker was one of them. Or was somewhere else."

Shapiro nodded. He was shuffling, reading, copies of the reports turned in, through channels, by members of the precinct squad who had found people, and asked questions of people, the night before. According to Florinda James, cook, Mrs. Singleton put money in the drawer every Saturday. There was no fixed amount put in but it was not ever an especially large amount. "What she had loose in her purse," Mrs. James had told the detective. It was usually, but not always, in small bills. How much was likely to be in the drawer at any given time? Maybe a hundred dollars. Maybe not more than fifty.

"Baker could have thought there was a lot more," Cook said. "Of course, so could the kid."

"You can get into the house through the basement," Shapiro said. "Go upstairs into the kitchen. Or go out and up two or three steps into the garden. Baker wouldn't have had to go through the garden and be seen by his son. Looks as if somebody is going to have to ask around at hardware stores which make keys, doesn't it, Tony?"

"Give the precinct boys something to do," Tony Cook said. "They —"

The telephone rang on Shapiro's desk and Shapiro spoke his name into it. He listened. He said, "She there now, Lieutenant?"

Cook could hear the answer. It was, "Yeah. With her father."

"We'll sit in," Shapiro said, and put the receiver back and stood up.

"Girl showed up at Charles Street," he told Cook. "Says she was with Roy yesterday afternoon. At the Singleton house. In the garden. And — that she went with him when he went up to thank Mrs. Singleton. And that Mrs. Singleton was dead when they got there."

Cook said he'd be damned.

"Yes," Shapiro said. "You and me, Tony. Let's get along."

VIII

Shapiro identified himself to the desk sergeant at Charles Street. He said, "This girl who says she was with young Baker yesterday?"

The girl was in the squad room with Lieutenant Mulligan. And, the sergeant said, with her father. And the squad room was that way.

In the squad room, Mulligan was sitting at a desk in a corner. A man in a blue suit was sitting at one end of the desk, with a window behind him and a notebook on the desk in front of him. On wooden chairs, facing Mulligan across the desk, were a gray-haired man with very square shoulders and a girl with long blond hair — soft hair which rippled to her shoulders. Mulligan said, " 'Lo," with no marked enthusiasm to Shapiro and Tony Cook. Then he said, "Get yourselves chairs if you want to."

They got themselves chairs and found space for them around the desk, Shapiro where he could see the girl who had, from Mulligan's grumpy attitude, thrown a monkey wrench into the machinery. She was a very pretty girl and looked to be sixteen or so. She had blue eyes, and above them her forehead, very white, rose straight to the soft hair. It was the kind of forehead which makes some women look innocent as long as they live, almost as if they always remained, in essence, babies.

The man beside her had a long rigid face, and it was set sternly. He looked sternly at Shapiro and Cook as they pulled chairs up, making a narrow circle about the desk.

"My daughter," the man said, "has told you what she insisted on telling. I see no reason why she should be required to tell it again." He looked even more sternly at Lieutenant Nathan Shapiro.

"Mr. Raymond Franklin," Mulligan said. "And his daughter Ellen. This is Lieutenant Shapiro. And —" He looked at Cook and shrugged heavy shoulders. Cook gave his name. Mulligan repeated it after him. "Detective Anthony Cook." Franklin looked unrelentingly at Shapiro and at Cook. He did not say anything to either of them. But the girl said, "Please, Father. I want to tell them whatever they want to know. Because Roy is my *friend* and they're making a dreadful mistake. A perfectly *dreadful* mistake."

The girl's voice was light and very young.

When she said "*dreadful* mistake" tears came into her eyes and she blinked at them. She had long eyelashes, darker than her hair. Her face was soft with youth, as her voice was soft. But her cheekbones were evident under the softness and the delicate bones of her jaw gave definition to the young face.

"Says she was with the Baker kid yesterday," Mulligan said. He had a heavy, grating voice. "Watching him garden. And — go ahead and tell them, Miss Franklin. What you told me."

"Roy and I are friends," the girl said. "And he knows how I am about flowers."

"About flowers?" Shapiro said.

"I love them," the girl said. "Simply love them. And where we live there aren't any, of course."

"Lower Fifth," Mulligan said, and gave an address. The address would put the Franklins very close to the Square. Close to the square the apartment houses on the east side of the avenue are new and large — and, Shapiro thought, expensive.

"You go to Clayton High?" Shapiro asked the girl.

"It's her mother's idea," Franklin said. "Some nonsense about her meeting all kinds of boys and girls her age. My wife is very democratic."

He spoke with what sounded like forced forbearance. His voice was gritty, like his face.

"Met Roy there?" Shapiro said and then, while the girl nodded her head so that the heavy blond hair swayed around it, "About yesterday, Miss Franklin?"

"It wasn't the only time," the girl said. "Roy told me about Mrs. Singleton's garden and how pretty it was and I asked him if he'd take me with him sometime. He didn't see why not, and so when the tulips were first out he let me go with him. That was a Sunday too. He said he didn't think Mrs. Singleton would mind and that anyway she probably wouldn't be there, because she mostly wasn't on Sundays. We went in through the basement, but that was all right, and the tulips were lovely. Just lovely. Yellow and white and some of them striped red and white."

"Yesterday?"

"What he said were annuals," the girl said. "I don't know the names of them. Sometime I'm going to have a garden of my own and grow all —"

"We plan to buy a place in the country," Franklin said. "The city is becoming almost —" he paused for a moment — "intolerable," he said. "Not in the least the way it was when I was young."

It is difficult to keep people on the subject.

It is a difficulty to which policemen become accustomed.

"Yesterday?" Shapiro said, with sad patience. "About yesterday, Miss Franklin?"

Pinned to it, the girl was succinct.

She had not gone with Roy Baker. "Because I had to go to this luncheon with Mother." But she had gone about four o'clock, and had rung the basement bell and Roy had come and let her in and they had gone to the garden and she had sat on a bench and looked at flowers and watched Roy work among them. "Oh," she said, "and we talked."

She didn't know how long she had watched the tall boy working in the garden. "Cultivating, they call it." She thought it might have been about an hour. Then Roy said, "That does it, Ellie." ("He calls me Ellie. Because we're friends.") He had also said that, after he picked up his money, he would walk her home.

"We went into the kitchen," the girl said. "And there were two envelopes on the table and money in both of them."

"That was in the papers," Mulligan said. "What Baker claimed. You read about this in the papers, Miss Franklin? What the kid says about money in envelopes?"

"I saw them," Ellen Franklin said. "Just like I say. Daddy, why don't they believe me?"

136

Franklin didn't say anything.

"You tell anybody about this, Miss Franklin?" Mulligan asked her. "Your father? Your mother?"

"I guess not. Father — he doesn't like me to what he calls get mixed up in things. Do you, Daddy?"

"No," Franklin said. "I do not, Ellen."

"So I didn't tell anybody," the girl said. "Because I didn't know they were going to say these dreadful things about Roy."

"Two envelopes," Shapiro said. "He opened them?"

"One of them had something written on it," the girl said. "When he opened that one he said, 'Gee, she's wonderful.' Something like that, anyway. And then that he'd go up and leave her a note or something to thank her."

"Which also was in the papers," Mulligan said, to nobody in particular. "What he said."

"He suggest you go up with him?" Shapiro asked the girl.

He had not. But, "I'd read about the house and I thought it would be all right if I went with him and saw it myself. And he said he guessed it would be all right. It's a beautiful house. So — so big and everything."

"It is a beautiful house," Shapiro said. "You went upstairs with him?"

Suddenly, then, the girl leaned forward and

137

covered her face with her hands. She began to shake her head, and her slender body shook.

Her father put a hand on one of the shaking shoulders.

"I can't talk about it," the girl said. "It was so dreadful. I —"

Her voice was choked.

"Ellen," her father said, "it was what you insisted you had to do. Had a duty to do. A responsibility. Your mother and I accepted that. However unpleasant it might turn out to be."

He looked at Mulligan and then at Shapiro. "However unpleasant," he said, his voice scratching.

"You went upstairs with Roy," Shapiro said. "Tell me about the stairs, Ellen."

"I don't know what you mean about the stairs," Ellen said. "Just — stairs. Wide stairs. I mean the stairway was wide."

"Yes," Shapiro said. "You went up the stairs with him. Then?"

She pressed her fingers to her forehead. Her body moved with the deepness of the breath she drew in. When she spoke, she spoke very rapidly.

"He said," Ellen Franklin told them, "he'd call first, because she might have got home. He said, 'Mrs. Singleton?' and then said it again, a little louder. And then he knocked at the door and when he knocked it opened. And there she — she —" Again she moved her head from side to side, apparently in rejection. "She was lying on the floor," Ellen said. "And there was — I guess it was blood on — on the rug and —"

She stopped again. They waited this time.

"Roy ran in," Ellen said. "I stayed there at the door. He got down on his knees beside her and then he said, 'Ellie, she's hurt. Dead, maybe. Anyway, it's awful.' And then he started to turn — to turn her over on her back and then he said, speaking very loud, 'Go home, Ellie. You mustn't get mixed up in this. Go *home!*"

"And?" Shapiro said.

"I felt all sick," the girl said. "I just went down the stairs — and — and back into the kitchen, I guess. And out through the basement. I kept feeling I was going to be sick. All the way home I felt that way." She lifted her head, then. "When I got home I was," she said. "Dreadfully, dreadfully sick. It was all so — so awful. The way she looked and — the blood and everything. And —"

She stopped speaking and, again, covered her face with her hands.

"We're having the kid brought over," Mulligan said. "See what he says about all this. On account of it's sort of funny he didn't say anything about Miss Franklin here being with him."

The girl looked up and looked at Mulligan.

"He wanted to keep me out of it," she said. "That's why he told me to go home. So that I wouldn't —" She ended that with a shake of her head. "Maybe," she said, "he'll say I wasn't there at all. That I'm making it up."

"He's that kind of boy?" Shapiro asked her. "A boy who would keep you out of it even if it was bad for him?"

"Yes. Oh, *yes*. He's a wond —"

They waited for her to finish the obvious word. She did not.

"While you were in the garden with him," Shapiro said, "did he go into the house at any time?"

"No," she said. "Not ever. Not ever once."

Franklin stood up, then. He was a long, lean man with thin, square shoulders.

He said, "That's all you want of her, isn't it?" and spoke to Mulligan. "She's a child. She's had about all she —"

He stopped because Mulligan was moving his heavy head from side to side.

"No," Mulligan said, "like to have her repeat this with the boy here."

"You'll — force her to stay?"

Mulligan looked at Shapiro.

"No," Shapiro said. "If you mean physi-

140

cally, no, Mr. Franklin. If you want to take her home now, you can. No charge against her. We can bring the boy over to your apartment, if you'd rather have it that way. Because we do have to see what he says to this. You understand that, don't you?"

Franklin sat down again. They waited. They did not have long to wait. While they waited, Ellen Franklin put her folded arms on Mulligan's desk and put her head down on them.

A patrolman brought Roy Baker into the squad room. Baker wore a white shirt, open at the throat. He wore a blue denim jacket which fitted lumpily over his shoulders, which he held back resolutely. A little too resolutely, Shapiro thought. He was bracing himself. And he looked very young; as young as the girl who did not, at first, lift her head.

"Baker," the patrolman said, making the obvious clear to everybody.

The girl lifted her head then and turned in her chair and looked up at the tall boy. She said, "Hello, Roy," and her voice was uncertain.

The boy said, "Hello, Ellie."

"I've told them, Roy," Ellen Franklin said, and she began to hurry her words. "I've told them everything about it. I —"

Roy Baker stood erect and looked down at

her and they all — all except the police stenographer in the blue suit — looked up at him. They saw his eyebrows go up and his head move, almost jumpily, from side to side.

"Told them what?" Roy said. "Everything about what?"

His voice had been warm, had had brightness in it, when he said hello to the girl. Now it was distant, without inflection.

"About yesterday," the girl said, and again spoke rapidly. "About my being in the garden with you and going upstairs with you and that after I got there at four o'clock — only it was earlier than that, really — you didn't go into the house at all and —"

"Ellie," the boy said in the same detached voice, "I don't know what you're talking about. You mean Mrs. Singleton's garden?"

"No, Roy," the girl said. "You mustn't any more. Because, I've told them, Roy. Just the way it happened."

They kept on looking up at the tall boy. He shook his head again. He said, "I don't get it, baby. I sure don't get it. What would you be doing in the garden? I don't get it." He shook his head again.

"You don't want to get me mixed up in anything so — so awful," Ellen said. "That's why you say that. But, don't you see, I *am* what you call mixed up in it. And if you

142

didn't go into the house from before four — maybe it was around three-thirty really — until we both went in and found her, you couldn't have — have done anything to her."

"Ellie," the boy said, "you're a crazy kid. Just crazy, baby."

With that, the warmth came back into his young voice. He moved a step forward and, Shapiro thought, started to reach out toward her. His shoulders moved under the lumpy jacket. But then he stopped. He looked around at the men who looked at him. He ended by looking at Raymond Franklin. He said, "You're her father, sir?"

Franklin said, "Yes," his voice scratching the word out.

"Whyn't you take Ellie home, sir?" the boy said. "She's — she's just a kid." He looked at Ellen then and he said, "I love you. But you're just a kid."

As he said that, color surged up under the gardener's tan of his face.

The girl looked up at him and color surged in her face, as it had in his.

"You never said that before," she said. "Never before."

She started to get up from her chair. As she turned it from the desk the chair grated on the floor. She was half up, facing the boy

— most evidently on her way to the boy — when her father reached to her shoulder and pressed her back onto the chair. He said, "You've done enough already, Ellen."

She looked up at Shapiro. She sat tensely on the wooden chair, but did not try again to stand. Her father's hand stayed on her shoulder, pressing down on it.

"Don't you see, sir," the girl said to Shapiro, "He's still just trying to keep me from being mixed up in — in something so ugly. Whatever happens to him. Because — you just heard what he said?"

"Yes, Ellen," Shapiro said. "I heard what he said."

"Then it's because — because of that — that he's — that he doesn't care what happens to him as long as I —"

Shapiro's long face did not change. He did not shake his head. But the girl stopped speaking and merely looked up at him. There was, he thought, anxiety in her face — anxiety and a kind of eagerness.

"Do you feel the same way about him?" Shapiro asked her.

It was surprise in her face this time.

"Why, of course," Ellen Franklin said. "Of course. For months and *months*."

Roy again started to reach out toward the girl, but Franklin stood up.

144

"Leave her alone, boy," Franklin said, and his voice scratched again. "Just leave her alone."

He pulled his daughter up from the chair and he looked around at Mulligan, at Shapiro and at Cook.

"I," Franklin said, "am taking my daughter home. Whatever any of you say."

Mulligan looked at Shapiro and raised heavy eyebrows.

"Yes, I think so," Shapiro said. "For now, anyway."

"Roy," the girl said. "*Roy!* You mustn't —" Her light young voice went up. It strained at the words. But her father had pushed her across the room, by then, and to the door and had reached around her and pushed the door open. He kicked the door closed after them.

"Well, Roy?" Shapiro said.

"She's my girl," Roy said. "I want her to be my girl. But she's all crazy mixed up."

"She wasn't in the garden with you yesterday?"

"No. She's just trying —"

"Yes," Shapiro said, "it may be that way. Did you ever take her into the Singleton garden when you were working there? To show her the flowers?"

"Once," Roy said. "Maybe two-three weeks ago. So she could see the tulips."

"Ask Mrs. Singleton if it would be all right?"

"Yes. I asked her. And she said, 'Flowers are meant to be looked at, boy.' So I knew it would be all right."

"You want anything else from Baker?" Mulligan said across the desk.

"Not right now," Shapiro said.

Mulligan got up and from behind his desk and took the tall, blond boy by the arm and across the room to the door. He opened the door and said, into the corridor, "O.K. Take him back." Mulligan came back and sat down at the desk again.

"Lying for him," he said. "These kids nowadays. Crazy. Can't believe anything they say."

"Maybe it's that way," Shapiro said. "Only, you'd think he'd have jumped at it, wouldn't you? Said, sure she was there. Because if it's the way she said it was, he couldn't have killed Mrs. Singleton, could he? Because the M.E.'s man says she was killed not earlier than around four-thirty and they don't slip up much."

"Only the kid didn't," Mulligan said. "Because, maybe, he figured we weren't believing her anyhow and thought it would make him look good if he didn't back her up. See what I mean?"

"Yes," Shapiro said, and stood up. "Rejection of offered sacrifice. Because if it came to court and she stuck to this, and it could be proved a lie, she'd be in for a perjury charge. Could have been that. You'll check the girl out? Find out where she was yesterday? Because if she thought she could get away with this story of hers, she wouldn't have been home, would she? Because she's a bright kid, Lieutenant."

"Oh," Mulligan said, "yes, I guess we've got to. Though, for my money, this doesn't change anything." He looked at the ceiling, apparently for further words. "What they call romantic," Mulligan said. "Romantic gesture. That's what they call it."

The familiar words came uncertainly from Lieutenant Mulligan's heavy lips.

"All the same, I'm not buying the girl's story," Cook said, as they walked away from the station house, and toward the nearest subway station. "You buying it, Nate?"

"Apparently he had taken her there before," Shapiro said. "I don't think into the house. The staircase is quite a job, Tony. Would have made an impression, particularly on a pretty and, like Mulligan says, romantic girl. Didn't on her."

"So," Cook said, "we end up where we've been all the time, don't we?"

"Not entirely," Shapiro said. "If she sticks

147

to the story — if Mulligan's boys don't find anything to make it come unstuck — a jury might believe her, Tony. And if the kid has any kind of a lawyer, the lawyer won't let the kid go on the stand to deny the girl was there."

"He told us. Mulligan's steno took it down."

"In," Shapiro said, "the absence of the boy's lawyer. Let's give this Gage guy another buzz and if we don't get him call it a day."

They didn't get him. Nathan Shapiro took the subway home to Brooklyn and walked familiar streets to a familiar apartment. He smiled down at a familiar face, which had never, in a real sense, become familiar to him — which to him, after years, remained delight. But his sad eyes did not smile at Rose.

"After you've eaten," Rose said. "Had a glass of that wine of yours."

He ate. Afterwards they sat side by side on a sofa and the air conditioning in the apartment hummed softly and Nathan Shapiro sipped from a glass of sweet red wine. Because it was, in a sense, as much her case as his, he told her about the boy and the girl. He told it with no comment, no judgment, in phrasing or inflection but when he finished Rose said, "Why don't you believe her, Nathan? Because they're babies and in love with each other?"

He was a little surprised at that because it

seemed a tangent. But when he thought for a moment he realized that it was not necessarily a tangent.

"Perhaps," he said. "That may enter into it. Only, I hadn't realized that kids were like that nowadays. Romantic, this Lieutenant Mulligan called it. As if he were quoting from another language."

"My dear," Rose said, "they aren't changed so much. Oh, in the way they talk. With the words they use changing, I sometimes think, from day to day. And many of them are bitter now, and the bitterness comes out more freely. Weren't you bitter at the world when you were very young, Nathan? Think it a mismanaged world?"

"Perhaps," Nathan said, and sipped his wine. "I didn't march in protest demonstrations. I didn't go around chanting. Neither did you. We were talking about something else, weren't we?"

"They fall in love," Rose said. "The way they always did. Phrase it differently when they talk about it. And are more direct about it. A lot of them are, anyway. They feel, I think, more — hurried. Less willing to wait. It seems to be always wartime nowadays, doesn't it? With — oh, with life to live all at once."

"These two kids. You think they're different? Some kind of Romeo and Juliet?"

She laughed at that and shook her head. She said, "Not that, Nathan. I don't know this girl — what's her name again?"

He told her the girl's name.

"Not anything about her," Rose said. "The boy. He reads a lot, I think. I wouldn't be surprised if he writes poetry. Oh, not Marvell. Nobody does any more and it's perhaps rather a pity. In another idiom. But the impulse may be the same, down underneath."

"Marvell?"

" 'Had we but world enough and time,' " Rose Shapiro told her husband. "To his reluctant mistress. Not that anybody could call Marvell a romantic, I suppose. In the technical sense. We're drifting, aren't we? But we often do, don't we?"

Shapiro said yes to that.

"If the girl wasn't there when she says she was," Rose said, "she's lying to protect him, isn't she? Romantically, because she's in love with him."

"Every so often," Shapiro said, "people lie to get their names in the papers. Even confess to things they haven't done."

"You think this Ellen is that kind of girl?"

"No. But I don't know, most of the time, what kind of people people are. You know that."

150

She smiled at Nathan, with both amusement and tenderness in her smile. He was looking at the empty fireplace they sat in front of, but he knew how she was smiling.

"And the boy can be lying to keep the girl out of — out of a bad thing," Rose said. "Out of trouble with rigid parents. Her father sounds rigid. Inflexible. Roy may think her parents would do something to the girl if she got mixed up in anything bad."

"Send her to a convent?" Nathan said, gravely.

"To what they call a select boarding school, more likely," Rose said. "Oh, I know you're joking, my dear."

"Her father came with her to the station house," Shapiro said. "Let her have her way about telling her story. Not pleased about it, at a guess. Probably tried to talk her out of telling it. But didn't, obviously, force her out of it. And, this boy of yours apparently didn't know Franklin. Know whether he and Mrs. Franklin are strict parents."

"Oh," Rose said, "the girl could have told him. Probably did; probably made a big thing out of it. The way kids do. My parents don't understand me. That sort of thing. Not that there may not be truth in it. A good many parents don't. I meet a good many parents. Part of the job. Why do you believe the boy and not the girl, Nathan? Really why?"

"Because," Shapiro said, "I don't think she's ever been in the Singleton house. Ever gone up those stairs. Because, dear, she'd remember that staircase, which is a very special sort of thing. Has a special sort of — grandeur, I guess the word is — you don't see any more. 'Just stairs. Wide stairs.' That's what she said when I asked her about them. She went, she says, to look at flowers because flowers are so pretty. She went up a grand staircase without noticing it? Without imagining elegant ladies coming down it a hundred years or so ago? Where's your romantic then, Rose?"

Rose said, "Hmm." She thought a moment. She said, "Uh-huh." Then she said, "So nothing will come of it? Of the girl's romantic gesture? You and this Lieutenant Mulligan will just forget about it? Wipe it off the record?"

"No," Shapiro said. "Oh, no, Rose. Because, whether she's lying or telling the truth, it's part of the case, now. No. Mulligan will tell the District Attorney's office, because they won't want to be surprised if — when — there's a trial. And the D.A.'s office will tell the defense attorney, which is the way the New York County D.A.'s office does things."

"And?"

"I don't know," Shapiro said. "But if I were the boy's lawyer, I'd go before the judge who fixed bail and ask for a reduction in bail. In view of the newly discovered circumstances. And the District Attorney's office would oppose reduction, but maybe not very hard."

"And?"

"Probably not make much difference if the judge did lower the bond," Shapiro said. "Because there isn't any money. Father's a grocery clerk. And, sometimes, delivery boy. And bondsmen don't put up their money without getting their share. So the boy'll probably stay —"

The telephone rang. Rose answered it. She said, "Yes, he is, Captain." She didn't sound happy about it and Nathan crossed the room and took the telephone from her, needing to be told nothing more than the change in his wife's voice had told him.

He listened. He said, "All right. I'll come over." He listened for a moment more. He said, "Well, she married a cop, Bill," and listened again. He said, "Mine to Dorian," and hung up.

He went to the shelf on which his service revolver lives when it is not attached to Lieutenant Nathan Shapiro. He began to strap it on.

"Man we've been trying to get hold of has showed up," Shapiro told Rose, and waited an instant. Rose said, "Damn," as was appropriate.

"And Bill Weigand sends his best," Shapiro said. "And says he's sorry."

Nathan Shapiro kissed his wife and put on his hat and went down to familiar streets and to a subway station which also is familiar. A familiar train took him away from where he wanted to be.

IX

Joseph Gage's apartment was the second floor of a house in the West Thirties. It was a well-kept-up house, Shapiro thought as he climbed white steps and turned a polished doorknob and selected the button he wanted from five buttons, each set in a polished brass plate. When he pressed the button, the door clicked at him almost at once, and he climbed a flight of carpeted stairs to a landing. The door he faced at the top of the flight was opened before he had time to ring the doorbell.

The man who stood in it was tall. He had smooth black hair and a lean, sharply defined face — deep-set eyes and bony nose and hard jaw lines. He also had a pointed black beard.

Shapiro said, "Mr. Gage?" and the man said, "Yes. You'll be Captain Weigand?"

His voice had volume; a little more volume, Nathan Shapiro thought, than was at the moment entirely needed. There was a word for that kind of voice, Shapiro thought. Not loud, actually. But carrying. "Projected" — that was the word for the voice. Shapiro, not projecting his own, said that he was not Captain Weigand and said who he was.

"Talked to Weigand," Gage said. "They told me he was the man to talk to. But all right. Come on in."

The room Shapiro went into was a high-ceilinged room with tall windows on the street side. The windows were closed and an air conditioner hummed.

"Well," Gage said, "you people found out who killed my wife? This kid there's a story about in the *Times?* Damned murdering kids. Sit down, why don't you?"

Shapiro sat down in a low, modern chair. The chair was so low that there was nothing to do with legs but stretch them out in front.

"The boy is a suspect," Shapiro said. "You called the captain. Wanted to tell us something?"

"Knew you people would want to talk to me," Gage said, and sat down in another low chair and stuck his legs out. He also stroked his pointed beard. "Nothing to tell you you don't know. She was my wife and she was lovely and some bastard killed her. You people suspect husbands the first thing, from what I've heard."

"Have you?" Shapiro said. "No. Want to talk to them, of course. Matter of fact, I've

156

been trying to get you on the phone most of the day."

"In a boat," Gage said. "Fishing. Out on Long Island I've got a shack and a boat. I rented a car yesterday morning and drove out and went fishing. Drove back this afternoon and went to the theater — plenty of time to change and put on make-up before I went on. And in the lobby there was a notice. 'This performance canceled,' the notice said. So I went around to the stage door and old Barny told me she'd been killed."

"The first you'd known of it?"

"It sure as hell was. After Barny told me, I came back here and read about it in the *Times*. It said that Captain William Weigand of the Homicide Squad was in charge, so I called this Weigand. Your boss, Lieutenant?"

"Yes," Shapiro said. "You don't listen to the radio much, Mr. Gage? Or read newspapers out on Long Island?"

"Out there," Gage said, "I fish."

"Have friends with you yesterday? Before you left to drive back to town?"

"Nobody. Oh, I get it. No. Nobody can say he was with me yesterday at — about when, Lieutenant?"

"Five o'clock or around then," Shapiro said. "Have you got a key to your wife's house, Mr. Gage?"

"So I could go in and kill her?"

"Just, have you got a key to the house. From what we hear, you and your wife were separated. It was her house."

"It sure as hell was her house. No, I didn't have a key. Gave mine back to her when — when we decided things weren't working out for us. Decided to take a breather. Think about things for a bit. You married, Lieutenant?" He paused for a moment. "Shapiro?"

Shapiro said yes.

"Ever want to take a vacation from your wife?"

Shapiro said no.

"Some do and some don't," Gage said. He pulled at his beard. He said, "Shave this damn thing off now with the show closed." Shapiro shook his head. "Had to grow it for the part," Gage said. "God knows why. But Les wrote a beard in."

"Lester Agee, you mean? One of Mrs. Singleton's former husbands?"

"The chap," Gage said. "He's one of the chaps you'd better talk to."

"I have," Shapiro said. "He's very broken up about Mrs. Singleton's death. That is, Mrs. Gage's death."

More than you seem to be, Shapiro thought, and did not say.

"Wants you to think so," Gage said. "The

only thing breaks Les up is third-act trouble. What did he tell you? About Jenny? And, at a guess, about me?"

"That you and your wife were separated. That she was planning a divorce. Or that you both were. Is that true?"

"Make any difference now? Now she's dead?"

"It might," Shapiro said. "Were you planning a divorce?"

"While back, yes," Gage said. "Week or so ago we decided not. Fact is, I was going to move back into the house this week. Something good old Les didn't know about. Unless she broke it to him, which maybe she did."

"Earlier today," Shapiro said, "he told me you and your wife were going to get a divorce. And — that he and she were going to remarry."

Gage laughed at that. He had, to Shapiro's ears a harsh laugh — a derisive laugh.

"The poor hopeful son of a bitch," Gage said. "Wasn't on the cards. Never had been. Oh, that she might go to Reno. Yes. But, as I just told you, that was out. Whatever Les Agee thought."

"Or," Shapiro said, "was told?"

Gage said he didn't get it. Then he said, "You mean Jenny told him that? Not like her, Lieutenant. Straight as a string, Jenny was.

That I'll say for her."

"Straight as a string" has always seemed an odd simile to Shapiro, who knows how strings can tangle. As, of course, can murder investigations.

"Always was," Gage added to what he had just said.

"By the way," Shapiro said, "you'd known Mrs. Singleton — I keep calling her that, but apparently everybody did — known her about how long, Mr. Gage?"

"Four or five years. We've been — had been — married a little over two years." He paused for a moment and pulled at the bothersome beard. "Four or five years I'd known her pretty well. Acted with her. In another way, I'd sort of known her most of my life. Who she was, if you get what I mean. As who didn't?"

"By the way," Shapiro said. "How old are you, Mr. Gage?"

"You want to know the damnedest things. Thirty-seven. And, sure if that's what you're getting at, she was maybe twenty years older. That what you're getting at?"

"Just getting the picture."

"Only," Gage said, and leaned up in the low chair and drew his legs in. "Only you're not. You're just counting years. And with her years didn't count. She was — what? Pretty near sixty?"

"You don't know?"

"Didn't come into it," Gage said. "Doesn't with women like Jenny was. Just knew she'd been pretty wonderful for a long time."

"According to *Who's Who*," Shapiro said, "she was fifty-eight."

"More than anybody I've ever known," Gage said, "she was what age she wanted to be. See her in *Always Good-bye?*"

"No, I never saw her."

"Woman of around thirty in the play," Gage said. "Young thirty. Face. Voice. Everything. I — hell, man, I felt old when we were on together. And that laughter of hers. Jesus, the way she could laugh!"

For the first time, to Shapiro's ears, Gage's voice had grief in it — grief and longing.

"Did you know, Mr. Gage, that Agee was paying her part of his royalties? Because, he says, the idea for this play was partly hers?"

"First time I ever heard of that," Gage said. "Not a hell of a lot like Les Agee. And she sure as hell didn't need it. Must have been a — oh, sort of a token thing."

"You knew she sometimes had ideas for plays?"

"Sure. Anyway, ideas for parts for her. Lots of us do in the profession. Do myself."

"Speaking of her not needing money," Shapiro said, "and of her having a lot of it. Know

161

anything about her will, Mr. Gage?"

"Wondered how long it would take you to get to that," Gage said. "Yes, I was in it. The way she changed it when we got married, anyway. Could be she's changed it again, couldn't it? After we decided on this vacation I told you about? Could have cut me off without a penny for all I know."

"Not quite," Shapiro said. "Dower rights. Unless some other arrangement was made? Some agreement?"

"Not that she told me about."

"Oh," Shapiro said, "you'd have known. Papers for you to sign. You knew that she and Mr. Agee remained friends. After you and she were married?"

"Of course. Why the hell not?"

"Saw each other rather frequently, the way I get it," Shapiro said. "As a matter of fact, they were going to have dinner together last night. So he says. And he did show up at the house. After the police got there. Around six, that was."

"So?"

"He says he didn't have a key to the house," Shapiro said. "You say you didn't have."

"That's right. About me anyway."

"You know Mr. Agee fairly well."

"Well enough. Arrogant so-and-so, for my money."

"Likely to be a violent so-and-so?"

"What's the idea? Giving me an out to see if I jump at it?"

"Just asking."

"No jump," Gage said. "Acted sometimes as if he thought he was God Almighty. Want me to say he'd go off his rocker if Jenny told him she and I were going to stay together? Go back together. So there wouldn't have been any remarriage. What you want me to say?"

"If that's what you think."

"No," Gage said. "That's not what I think. When he directed — sometimes he did his own plays — he'd yell at people. Most of them do. Think they know more about acting than actors."

"Happen to know whether he'd ever been an actor himself?"

"For a time, I think. Years ago. I never saw him act. Decided writing plays was a better bet. As God knows it is, if you happen to hit the way he did. Acting is a mug's game for most of us. Way the theater is nowadays, specially. Get roped in on a turkey and, nine times out of ten, that shoots the bloody season. For example — I'm out of a job now. Because they won't reopen *Always Good-bye*. Not without Jenny. So —" He shook his head.

"So?"

"Make the rounds," Gage said. "My agent

makes the rounds. Try out and try out. And maybe get a contract and rehearse for weeks and we have previews for two weeks and it opens on Tuesday and closing notices go up Saturday night. Like I said, it's a mug's game. Don't know why I ever got into it. Why any of us does. Unless it's just the itch."

"It doesn't," Shapiro said, "sound very steady work. You've been doing all right yourself, Mr. Gage?"

"Getting by," Gage said. "Scraping bottom some times, but not starving. Keeping up my Equity dues. And —"

Somewhere a telephone rang. Gage got up and moved lithely across the room. He said, "Hello?" and, "Yes, he is," and then, across the room, "Call for you, Lieutenant. Somebody must have known you'd be here."

"Seems like it," Shapiro said, and crossed the room to the telephone and said, "Yes, Captain?" He listened and said, "Can't say I'm surprised," and listened again and looked at his wrist watch while he listened. He said, "O.K., Bill. Maybe half an hour?"

When he went back, he did not again sit down in the low chair.

"About all, for now," Shapiro said. "Glad you got in touch with us, Mr. Gage. I guess —"

He stopped.

"One other thing," he said. "This kid —

Roy Baker — he says you interviewed him when he went to see Mrs. Singleton about the job. What did you think of him?"

"Seemed O.K.," Gage said. "Nice-looking kid. Jenny didn't mind nice-looking kids around."

"She was the one decided he'd do?"

"Yes. After all, it was her house. And her garden. But I thought the kid was all right. I'm not claiming I didn't. Looks now as if I was wrong as hell, doesn't it?"

"We don't know yet," Shapiro told him and said, "Maybe we'll want to talk to you again, Mr. Gage."

Gage slid up from his chair. He said he'd be around.

Shapiro was lucky in getting a taxi, which surprised him. It was a little less than half an hour after Bill Weigand, commanding, Homicide South, telephoned that Shapiro pushed a doorbell high up in an apartment house a block or so from the East River. Weigand opened the door and said, "Sorry about it, Nate. But it is yours. Right?"

From a deep chair in front of windows which overlooked the river, Dorian Weigand uncoiled, with a cat's fluid grace, and came up the room, a hand reached out. She said, "Hi, Nathan." He said, "Evening, Mrs. Weigand." "Dorian," Dorian Weigand said.

165

"Dorian," Nathan Shapiro said after her.

"Bill never takes time off," Dorian said. "Or lets other people. If you ever get home, tell your Rose we're sorry."

Shapiro said, "Sure," looking down into her green eyes as she coiled herself back into the deep chair. Her eyes always amazed him.

"Sherry?" Weigand said. "Right?"

"I don't —" Nathan said. "All right. Very small sherry."

He sat and looked at lights on the river until Weigand put a small glass of sherry on a table beside him. The glass was small but seemed to soar from its base.

"The D.A.'s office more than me," Weigand said and put his own glass, which did not contain sherry, on another table and sat in a chair by it. "About this girl who says she was with young Baker. Girl named Ellen Franklin. Right?"

"Yes."

"Point is," Weigand said, "do we believe her? What the D.A.'s office wants to know. Before court tomorrow. Or, do we believe the kid when he says she wasn't there?"

"Mulligan didn't waste any time," Shapiro said. "Getting through the D.A.'s office, I mean."

"Homicide Bureau," Weigand said. "Man named Simmons."

"Yes," Shapiro said. "I know Bernie Simmons. And?"

"You sat in," Weigand said. "Heard the girl. And heard the boy deny it. Which one do we believe, Nate? Because, Simmons says, it may make a difference. Because —"

Because the District Attorney's office, which in New York County is most scrupulous, had passed the information on to a man named Dunlap, court-appointed defense counsel. And Dunlap was going to court the next day, before the judge who had fixed bail at fifty thousand dollars, and ask the release of Roy Baker, held as a material witness. On the grounds of newly discovered evidence.

"Taking the girl to tell her story?"

"Actually," Weigand said, "taking Mulligan. To whom she went first. The point is, are we sure enough to tell the D.A.'s man to fight it? Or, fight reduction in bail, which is probably about all Dunlap hopes for? Mulligan, apparently, doesn't believe the girl's story and says you don't. Right?"

"I think," Shapiro said, "that she's been in the Singleton garden. Not necessarily yesterday or at the times she says. Which, incidentally, was four o'clock on the first time she told it and three-thirty later. I don't think she was inside the house. Above the basement. I don't think she went up with Baker and was there when he found the body. But I can't prove she wasn't. A jury might well believe her."

"Telling a lie for the boy's sake?" That was Weigand.

"For love's sake," Dorian said.

"Yes," Shapiro said. "I think she was — that it was what Mulligan brought himself to call a romantic gesture. But a jury might think the boy's denial she was there was the romantic gesture."

"We're a long way from a jury," Weigand said. "Why do you believe she wasn't in the house, Nate?"

"Because there's a pretty special staircase from the entrance hall to the second floor," Shapiro said. "What they used to call, I guess, a grand staircase. I've got no imagination. You know that. But I could damn near see elegant ladies in — oh, dresses with long trains or hoop skirts or whatever — coming down it. The girl loves flowers. Is maybe a romantic kid. Staircase didn't make any impression on her. Oh, that it was wide. Because, I think, she never saw it."

"Amounts to a hunch," Weigand said. "You don't believe the girl's story because of a staircase."

"I suppose it comes to that," Shapiro said. "Nothing to stick our necks out about. This lawyer Dunlap. Leak it to the papers?"

"Probably has already," Weigand said. "And — they'll jump at it, Nate. Young love sort of thing. Also, the girl's father is pretty well known. Patent lawyer. What they'll call a 'famed patent lawyer.' Daughter of famed patent lawyer alibis suspect in slaying of celebrated actress. Right?"

"Much too long for any headline I ever saw," Dorian said, speaking from the depth of the chair she curled in. "Also, can they call the boy a 'suspect'? Because, as I get it, he's merely a material witness."

Weigand raised his glass in her direction. He turned back to Shapiro.

"Have you and Cook found anybody who looks better?" he asked the sad-faced man. Shapiro shook his head. He took a sip from his glass of sherry. It was a little tart for his taste and he wondered what his stomach would make of it. His stomach is often petulant.

"We know the boy was there," Shapiro said. "That when he was picked up he had more money on him than we'd expect. And that there was no money in the drawer she kept it in. His explanation of that sounds a little spur-of-the-moment. He says he didn't see the cop on the beat and wasn't running away from him. But he was running. Nobody can blame precinct. He looks like a client. On the other hand —"

He paused. Weigand waited a moment. Then he said, "On the other hand, Rose as a character witness? Or, more than that, Nate?"

"There's a man named Agee," Shapiro said. "Says he was going to remarry Mrs. Singleton. There's a man named Gage who's married to her now — was until last night — who says he and the lady were going to go on with the marriage they had and that if Agee thought different he thought wrong. Agee seems to me a man who might get emotional if, say, he got his hopes up and somebody knocked them down."

"Emotional enough to use a knife?"

"Bill," Nathan Shapiro said and turned in his chair to face Weigand more directly, "I'm no good at guessing things like that. Specially about people like Agee. I don't know what makes people like that tick. They're beyond me. You ought to know that."

"And," Weigand said, gravely, "you have no imagination and are good only with a gun. I know about that."

"And," Dorian said, still a little absently, "when you get among people who're involved in the arts, you are all at sea. And helplessly drown in the sea."*

*When last working on a case which involved "people in the arts," as recounted in *Murder for Art's Sake*, Shapiro solved, not drowned. Dorian Weigand helped him.

170

"Oh," Shapiro said, "sometimes I get lucky. Which — misleads people."

"Sure," Weigand said. "Everybody knows about your luck, Nate. Emotional enough to use a knife? In your worthless opinion."

"He acted as if he had been very much in love with Mrs. Singleton," Shapiro said. "On the other hand, he had been an actor once, according to Gage. He may have been acting."

"Why?"

"I don't know. All right, I don't think he was acting. And, he was there — showed up at the house, I mean — an hour or two after she was killed. Identified himself. Appeared to be badly shaken up. It could be that he staged that. Could be he was there a couple of hours earlier. Could be he had a key, though he says he hadn't."

"Reasonable doubt? As far as the kid's concerned?"

"Could be made to sound like that, I guess. And there're a couple of others. Gage probably will get some, anyway, of her money. Of which there seems to be a lot. Gage was off by himself in a boat. Fishing. Didn't know anything about his wife's death until he went around to the theater this evening. He gave his key to the house back to her when they separated. Decided to take a vacation from each other, way he puts it. Maybe he did. And maybe he had the key copied before he did."

"And he profits. A hell of a lot more than the kid would from what he found in the lady's cash drawer."

"Yes. I did think of that. All right, another reasonable doubt, if you want to put it that way."

"He needs money?"

"Gave me a pitch about how precarious an actor's life is. Doesn't live as if he were broke."

"They'll close the show with the star dead," Weigand said. "Open it again with someone else?"

"Haven't decided, as I get it," Shapiro said. "General feeling seems to be they won't."

"Leaving Gage out of a job," Weigand said.

"And Mr. Agee out of royalties," Dorian said. "How does Mr. Agee live, Nate? He's had a lot of successes."

"Like he'd had a lot of successes," Shapiro said. "Big apartment in a high-rise. Big rent or big investment if he bought it. Won't be pinched, I think, if royalties from *Always Good-bye* dry up. He was giving Mrs. Singleton a cut on his royalties, incidentally."

"Why?" Weigand asked him. Shapiro told them why.

"Generous," Weigand said. "Two, now, beside the boy. Any more up your sleeve?"

"Cook's, actually," Shapiro said. "Went around to see the boy's father. Ralph Baker, the father is. In a jam — saloon brawl over Baker's wife — years ago. Cook recognized him. Grocery clerk. Sometimes delivery boy."

He told them the rest about Ralph Baker.

"Knew there was money lying around in the house," Bill Weigand said. "Guess it, anyway. May have guessed there was a lot more than there seems to have been. Could have got hold of the kid's key and had it copied."

"Knowing suspicion would be likely to fall on his son?" That was Dorian. "That kind of man, Mr. Cook think?"

"How can anybody tell?" Shapiro said. "All right, Cook wasn't much impressed by him. Type we run into pretty often, according to Cook. Who's run into a lot of them."

"Three reasonable doubts," Weigand said. "Any more in sight, Nate?"

"I don't know that it's reasonable," Shapiro said. "Another man we ought to talk to, maybe. Another husband. Apparently she walked out on him and —"

"Kurt Morton," Dorian said. "They were a famous husband-and-wife team. I haven't heard anything about him for years. He's still alive then, Nathan?"

"Seems to be," Shapiro said. "Sort of dropped out, from what they say. May think he was pushed out. By her. Could be he's brooded over it."

"A long brood," Dorian said. "A brood of years. Not really very reasonable, is it?"

"No," Shapiro said. "Just a man to talk to. Because murder itself isn't reasonable and you can't tell."

"Husbands," Dorian said. "And wives too, of course. Always the first in line, aren't they? The police always take such a dim view of marriage, it seems to me."

"From dim experience," Bill Weigand told his wife. "You'll see this Morton, Nate?"

"If we're going on with it," Shapiro said. "You said a couple of days. Because Rose had this hunch."

"Right," Weigand said. "An infectious hunch, isn't it, Nate? From her to you and you to me."

Shapiro looked sadly at his glass and sipped from it.

"Well," he said, "there are loose ends worth pulling at."

"Yes," Weigand said. "Very clear at first. You and Cook have fogged it up a little."

"I know," Nate Shapiro said and sighed. "What I'm best at."

"You do think the girl's lying?"

"The way it feels to me. For what that's worth."

"Oh," Bill Weigand said, "nothing, obviously. All the same —"

He got up and walked the length of the long living room to a telephone and spun its dial. He was answered quickly and said, "Bernie?" He spoke loudly enough for the two to hear him down the room. Clearly he got "Yes" for an answer.

"We're not sure enough for a big pitch on it, Bernie," Bill Weigand said. "Nate Shapiro has stirred up several reasonable doubts."

He listened for a moment.

"Right," Bill said. "He's very good, Bernie. Token resistance, maybe? Leading to a suitable compromise. Right? Because Nate thinks the girl probably is lying for the kid. And —"

Apparently he was interrupted. He listened for a moment, said, "I'll ask him," and covered the receiver with a hand and spoke down the room, his voice raised.

"Bernie," he said, "says, 'Because she thinks he's guilty?' You think that, Nate?"

Nathan Shapiro is, he feels, always being asked for opinions he knows are worthless.

"How do I know?" he said.

"You don't," Weigand said, still muting the receiver. "So guess, Lieutenant."

Shapiro hesitated.

"At a guess," he said, "that doesn't follow. Could be, she only thinks he's in trouble and needs to be helped." He paused for a moment. Then he said, "She's a child, Bill. I don't know anything about children."

"Right," Weigand said and took his covering hand from the receiver and spoke into it.

"Nate doesn't think the girl believes the boy is guilty," Weigand said. "Thinks she's an impulsive, romantic child." He listened for a moment. He said, "Oh, I know it doesn't prove anything. Isn't evidence of anything. You asked how sure we are. So, we're not sure. You'll have to take it from there, Bernie."

X

Criminal Court Judge Francis O'Brien would see counsel in chambers. He added, "You too, Lieutenant," and got up from the bench and went through a doorway behind it. Assistant District Attorney Henry MacKenzie and Clarence Dunlap, counselor at law, and police Lieutenant Patrick Mulligan went around the bench and through the door after him. Judge O'Brien was at his desk when they caught up. He had just lighted a cigarette. One of the trying aspects of being a presiding judge is that one cannot smoke on the bench.

"Application for the discharge of one Roy Baker," Judge O'Brien said. "Held in bail as a material witness in the fatal stabbing of one Jennifer Singleton. All right, Clare. Make your pitch."

"The kid couldn't have done the killing," Dunlap said. "His girl friend was with him all the time. Was with him when he found the body."

"She says," Lieutenant Mulligan said, with

177

heavy skepticism in his voice. "That's all it comes to. What the kid who's been looking at too many soap operas says. And he says she wasn't."

To this Judge O'Brien said "Hmmm." Then he said, "The District Attorney's office opposes, Mac? And, are you going before the grand jury?"

"Even," MacKenzie said, "if the girl is telling the truth, Baker's still a material witness. As for trying for an indictment, I don't know. Word hasn't come down. You know how the chief is about that sort of thing, judge."

"Very well," Judge O'Brien said. "Very well indeed, Mac. Also, I rather wondered why you didn't charge homicide in the first place. Assuming that the material witness thing is a gimmick. It is, isn't it?"

"At first," MacKenzie said, "it looked open and shut. We decided it wasn't yet, anyway."

"Because," Mulligan said, "the brain boys moved in and — all right, Mr. MacKenzie — the D.A.'s office came sort of unstuck."

"Not entirely," Judge O'Brien said. "Considering the amount of bond they asked for. And got. You really expect to get him discharged, Clare? Or will a reduction in bond satisfy you?"

"The material witness bit is a gimmick," Dunlap said. "We all know that. Not enough to make a homicide charge stick. So, just put the kid in storage while they dig up more. Yes, I'm applying for his discharge. Without bail."

The judge crushed his cigarette out and lighted another. He did not hurry with either action. Then he said, "Hmmm." Then he said, "You oppose that, Mac."

"Outright discharge, yes," MacKenzie said. "A reasonable reduction in bail — well, we might go along."

"The kid's father is a grocery clerk," Dunlap said. "There's no money. There's no security a bondsman would look at."

"If I fixed bond at, say, five thousand?" the judge said.

"A hundred to one," Dunlap said, "the kid stays in storage. Five thousand, fifty thousand. What's the difference? And he's a nice kid, Frank. I mean Your Honor. Locked up with a bunch of guys who aren't nice at all. When there's nothing on him except, for God's sake, he happened to be there. And —"

"Save it for the jury, Clare," Judge O'Brien said. "Would you oppose reduction to five thousand, Mac?"

"We'd go along on that," MacKenzie said.

"As a matter of public relations?" O'Brien said. "Or because the girl's story knocks the bottom out of your case? Considering who her father is? Or just because you agree with Clare here that five thousand or fifty thousand come to pretty much the same thing for the boy?"

"You'll have to ask the chief that," Mac-Kenzie said. "Or Bernie Simmons."

"You just came along to say the words?"

"The office of the District Attorney, New York County, does not oppose a reasonable reduction in the bond fixed for Roy Baker, held as a material witness," MacKenzie said. "It does oppose outright discharge of Baker." He paused for a moment. Then he said, "Your Honor."

"Very well," Judge O'Brien said. He pressed a button on his desk and, very quickly, the court clerk knocked and, told to come in, came in and said, "Your Honor?"

"Order for reduction of bond in re Roy Baker, held as a material witness," O'Brien said. "Draw it up for me to sign. The reduction is from the fifty thousand now set to five thousand."

"Thanks for nothing, Frank," Clarence Dunlap said.

But it did not turn out to be for nothing. At eleven o'clock that morning, Mrs. Raymond Franklin posted bail of five thousand dollars, by certified check, with the court clerk. By eleven-thirty, Roy Baker walked out of the House of Detention for Men. He went home and changed and still was in time, at Clayton High School, for his afternoon class in creative writing.

Shapiro checked in late at Homicide South. He had been out late the night before. One of the advantages of a lieutenant's rank is, within reason, leeway. That morning he felt no urgency. He was vaguely disappointed that he did not, but he was not surprised. A man, detective or other man, feels urgency when he is going somewhere and knows where he is going. Nathan Shapiro was not and did not.

Routine suggested Kurt Morton, second husband of Jennifer Singleton. A man, possibly, with a grudge. But with, as Dorian Weigand had pointed out, a very aging grudge. Morton, Shapiro thought gloomily, would turn out to be a dead-end street. If he could find the street.

There was a catch in that. The Manhattan directory listed some columns of Mortons but only one of them had "Kurt" as a first name. And that Kurt Morton had an address in Harlem and was listed as "Morton, Kurt, b" which was not encouraging. Shapiro dialed the number anyway and got "Yeah?" for an answer. Mr. Morton? He got, "You're late, man. Dead two years." It didn't matter, after that, but Shapiro has curiosity, which is essential in his profession. The nature of the late Mr. Morton's business? "What is this, anyhow?"

"Just wondered," Shapiro said. "Looking for another Morton, probably."

"Guess you are, man. We're men's furnishings here. Want to buy some shirts, maybe?"

There are many trivial annoyances in the trade Shapiro follows; many small and scratchy details.

There was no Kurt Morton at all in the Brooklyn directory, although there were three who were merely "Morton, K." The Bronx and Queens directories got him no further, unless he — or Cook — were to check out all the "Morton, K's." There must be a quicker way to find this dead-end street. Then it came to Shapiro. Around something called The Players a good deal, a man named Temple had told Cook. A club of some sort, apparently. Shapiro looked it up and found a listing for "Players, The" on Gramercy Park, South. He dialed the number.

Mr. Kurt Morton was a member of The Players. More, he was staying at The Players. Whether he was at the moment in the club —

"Rather important I get in touch with him," Shapiro said.

Mr. Morton's room could be tried. It was tried. Mr. Morton did not appear to be in it. If it was really important — a part perhaps?

— Mr. Morton almost always lunched at the club. A message could be left for Mr. Morton at the bar. Or —

"Wait a minute. I'll step out and have a look."

Shapiro waited a little less than a minute.

"Just came down," the man at The Players said. "Should I ask him to come to the telephone?"

"Will he be there long, would you think?"

"Well," the man at The Players said, "I shouldn't wonder, Mr. —?"

Shapiro did not supply a name.

"An hour or so at a guess," the man said. "Mr. Morton is, I believe, at liberty just now. Er, between engagements. If it's about a part I'm sure he'd be glad —"

"I may catch him there," Shapiro said, and said, "Thanks," and hung up. The man at the club was surprisingly forthcoming. Possibly Morton, who was "between engagements," had asked him to be.

Nathan Shapiro was half up from his desk to start a cross-town walk to Gramercy Park when Bill Weigand came out of his office, looked around the squad room and said, "Oh, Nate. Come in a minute. Right?"

Shapiro went in.

"Young Baker's bond's been reduced," Weigand told him in the small office. "From

183

fifty grand to five. And, it's been posted, Nate. Want to guess who posted it?"

"I'm no good at guessing," Shapiro said.

"Mrs. Franklin. Mrs. Raymond Franklin. The mother of the girl you don't believe, Nate. Because Ellen begged her to? Because Ellen thinks he's a cat who's out of sight?"

"A —" Shapiro said and then, "Oh. It could be, Bill."

"Or," Weigand said, "because she believes her daughter, without being begged to? And, maybe, thinks we're being too tough on a boy her baby is crazy about? A guy who's groovy."

"I don't know."

"Interesting, sort of, it should be Mrs. Franklin who came up with the bond money. Not her husband."

"Yes," Shapiro said. "But Franklin was, I think, against his daughter's telling this story of hers at all. And, doesn't approve of the girl's going to public school and mixing around with all sorts of kids."

" 'Bow, bow, ye lower middle classes'?"

"At a guess. It was the mother, according to Franklin, who insisted on Ellen's going to Clayton High. I gathered Franklin didn't approve. Just went along."

"Five thousand," Weigand said, "is a good deal to stake on a kid you don't know anything about."

"Maybe it isn't a good deal to her," Shapiro said. "But I don't see that it ties in to anything, do you?"

"No," Weigand said. "Not even a loose end. But we might —"

"Oh, yes," Shapiro said. "I'll ask her why she's decided to be a fairy godmother. After I see a man about a part."

Weigand raised eyebrows. Shapiro told him about Kurt Morton and his own impression — which probably was mistaken — that Morton had feelers rather anxiously out for a job. "Because," Shapiro said, "not that I know anything about clubs, but this guy at The Players — manager or whatever — was very outgoing about Morton's being between engagements."

"So?"

"So nothing, probably. Only, if he's been out of work for a long time, and badly needs to get a part, it might make him — well, broody. Broody over better days and, could be, bitter about the woman who ended them."

"A hunch, Nate?"

"Just curiosity," Nate Shapiro said. "Like we've all got, Bill. Like the book says we're supposed to have."

"Right," Bill Weigand said. "Go satisfy it, Nate."

Heat had settled on New York and the air

was heavy. The air caught in the throat and in the lungs. There had been a breeze at the start of the day, but the breeze had given it up.

Nathan Shapiro walked across town in the heat to see a man who might bear a grudge.

A detective does a lot of walking, shoe soles rasping on cement. He climbs stairs and rings doorbells and asks questions and most of the answers to his questions get him nowhere. Tony Cook had started early at doorbell ringing and so had Detective (2nd gr.) Lawrence Simpson, also of Homicide, Manhattan South. And so, cooperating, had Detectives Holmes and Watson, of the precinct squad. Holmes and Watson often worked as a team. Somebody had once thought it appropriate.

They shared the houses in Hunter Street, which ran a block north of the part of Van Allen Street which is called Point Street. Rear apartments on Hunter Street, in that block, have windows from which anyone with enough interest, and time on his hands, can look across back yards at what goes on in rear apartments in Point Street.

The building on Hunter Street which was directly opposite the Singleton house reached up ten stories into, that day, murky air. On each floor there were two rear apartments. Holmes and Watson rang twenty doorbells.

Eight of them were not answered.

People are, reasonably enough, suspicious of men who come around asking questions. People, reasonably enough, want to see badges. It all takes time. It is generally a waste of it.

"We weren't home Sunday. Weekends in the summer we mostly go to the country. It's lovely in the country this time of year. Up in Putnam County we have a little place — just a cabin, really — and Tom gets to play tennis and —"

That was a blond young woman in shorts and halter, answering Ralph Watson, who was in a somewhat wrinkled gray suit, and who said, "Yes'm. Must be nice in the country. Sorry to have bothered you."

"It hasn't been any bother, really," the blond young woman said. "I'm just sorry we can't help. It was such a dreadful thing to happen. And right over there, too."

She went to a window and looked out of it; looked down at a fenced place where flowers grew. "And to think," she said, "all the time we've lived here we didn't know the house over there was Mrs. Singleton's!"

"Think we've got nothing to do but watch our neighbors?" a man on the seventh floor asked Detective Arthur Holmes. "Anyway, we were at a movie Sunday afternoon. Had a late lunch and went to a movie. Didn't get back until around six."

"Why, yes," a rather sagging woman on the sixth floor told Detective Holmes. "I often look down at Mrs. Singleton's garden. It's so nice to see things kept *up* for a change. It's so nice to see *flowers* in the city."

"Sunday afternoon?"

"When was Sunday?"

Holmes told her when Sunday had been. She said, "Of course. Wasn't it a dreadful thing? About poor Mrs. Singleton, I mean?"

Holmes agreed it was a dreadful thing. Had she seen, Sunday afternoon, a young man working in the garden? And had she, perhaps, seen him go into the house at any time and come out of it again? About — oh, say about four-thirty? And had she seen anybody else with him in the garden? A girl, maybe?

"Sunday?" she said. "Oh, Sunday — of course. My bridge club was meeting here. Eight of us, you know. From about three — except that Mrs. Bridges was late and that held us up, because it's duplicate, actually — until it must have been after six. And of course, because I was the hostess, I had to do the tea and things. You know how it is."

"Play poker myself," Holmes said, more or less involuntarily. "But sure, I see how it was. No time to be looking out windows."

Holmes and Watson met on the sidewalk in front of the apartment house. They compared blanks. The residents of the Hunter Arms had been inattentive to activities of their neighbors on Sunday afternoon, when they had been home that Sunday afternoon.

"One guy on the tenth floor," Holmes said, "I wouldn't put past using binoculars. But he says he was at the ball game Sunday."

They separated; went to the buildings on either side which adjoined the Hunter Arms and also had rear windows. Neither of them expected much to come of it.

Tony Cook and Larry Simpson rang doorbells of houses which adjoined the landmark mansion which had been Jennifer Singleton's. A maid in a black uniform answered the doorbell Cook rang. The family had gone to the country for the summer. Yes, she had been there Sunday afternoon. Watching TV. And if she hadn't been, did they think she'd have been spying on the neighbors?

"Hear anything from the house next door?"

"I told you, I had the TV turned on. Like what?"

"A woman crying out," Cook said. "A woman screaming?"

"From next door," she said, "we don't never hear anything. I'll say that for these old houses. The walls are thick."

The middle-aged couple who lived in the house on the other side of the Singleton house had been in it Sunday. And they had sat for a while on their balcony, which, at an angle, overlooked Jennifer Singleton's garden. But that had been when they were having drinks before lunch. "We do on Sundays. It's rather a special thing for Kenneth and me."

From about one until a little after two they had been on their balcony. Yes, they had seen a young man working in the garden next door. A young man with blond hair? An all-right-looking boy, really. Was *he* the one? He looked — oh, so nice and clean. So different from a lot of the kids one saw around. Was he *really* the one who did it?

"We're trying to find out," Simpson told her. "There wasn't a girl with him while you were on the balcony?"

"No. Just the boy."

"And later. Did you and your husband happen to look out later?"

They had not. After drinks and lunch they had taken naps. "We usually do on Sundays. Unless we go out, of course. Or have friends in."

They had heard nothing? At, say, around five? Nothing from the house next door?

"It was warm," Mrs. Kenneth Lambert said. "We had closed the windows and turned

190

the air conditioning on. And, anyway, our bedrooms are on the street side."

A lot of steps to take on gritty cement in increasing heat. A lot of doorbells to ring. As, dividing the job, they went from house to house on the south side of Point Street, moving away from the Singleton house, the chance of turning up anything grew fainter. They needed a miracle — needed, for example, someone who had been walking home late on a Sunday afternoon and had seen somebody go into the Singleton house at around four or four-thirty, through front door or basement door. Seen somebody who could be described. Seen a girl going to the basement door, and a boy meeting her there and letting her in. Seen a man or a woman using a key to open that door, or the front door. Nobody was passing miracles for policemen.

They met again in mid-block, where two narrow houses faced the house in which Jennifer Singleton had died. Numbers 277 and 279, the houses were. Cook went up three scrubbed white steps at No. 277 and rang the doorbell.

He did not need to wait long. A blue-eyed girl of about twelve opened the door. She had blond hair to her shoulders and she looked a little, Cook thought, like the Tenniel drawings of a girl named Alice. Of course, Alice did not wear shorts and a halter. The child looked up at Cook and shook her head and the blond hair swayed on her shoulders with the movement.

"Grandfather says we don't want any," the girl said and started to close the door. Cook stopped it with a foot and said, "Any what?"

"Any anything," the girl said. "Brushes or books or anything. I want to close the door."

"No brushes," Cook said. "No books. I'm a detective. I want to ask some questions."

"Nobody's done anything," the girl said. "Go away."

"Your mother?" Cook said. "Or father or — or anybody?"

"They don't live here," the child said, with impatience in her young voice. "They're in South America. Almost all the time they're in South America."

"Who does live here?" Cook asked her.

"It's my grandfather's house," the girl said. She tried again to push the door shut and again Cook's foot stopped it.

"You and your grandfather," Cook said. "Who else, sister?"

"You're nosy," the child said. "What do you mean you're a detective?"

"Just that," Cook said. "And we're paid to be nosy, young lady. You and your grandfather and —"

192

"Grandfather's nurse, of course. And there's Amy. That's all who live here when mother and father are in South America, as they mostly are. Annie comes in twice a week to help with the cleaning but she doesn't count. Not really. Not that she isn't nice. You don't look like a detective to me. Not like the ones on television."

"I'm sorry," Cook said. "I'd like to talk to —"

A voice interrupted him. It was a strong, deep voice and came down from above.

"Who're you talking to, girl?" the man with the deep voice said.

The girl turned away, and as she turned pulled the door open. Cook looked into an entrance hall with a flight of stairs rising at the end of it. The voice, he thought, had come down the stairs from probably, the floor above.

"He says he's a detective," the girl said. "That's what he says, grandpa."

"Tell him we don't want —" the man with the deep voice said and then, "What do you mean a detective?"

"That's what —" the girl began and Cook stepped into the entrance hall and raised his voice. He said "Police detective, sir. About the murder across the street. Just part of the routine inquiry, sir. To see if anybody — any

193

of the neighbors — saw or heard any —"

"Elizabeth," the man upstairs said, "bring him up here. No, wait. Tell him to show you his badge, if he's a policeman."

"He says —" the child who was named Elizabeth, not Alice, told Cook. He had his badge out by then and held it toward her, cupped in his hand. She looked and took it out of his hand and turned it over and looked at the other side. Then she gave it back.

"It does," she said up the stairs, "say 'New York Police Department.' And there's a number on it. I guess maybe he's a policeman."

"All right," the man said. "Bring him up."

Elizabeth said, "Come on," and started up the stairs and Cook went on after her. He went after her through an open door and into a room on the street side which was the width of the narrow house. Sunlight came through windows which reached from floor to ceiling. Shafts of sunlight lay on a polished floor. In the middle of the big room there was a man in a wheel chair. He was, Cook thought, very old. He had a round pink face and his white hair shone. A very clean white blanket covered his legs.

He wheeled the chair nearer Cook and looked up at him. He said, "Let me see your badge, officer," and reached a hand out. He had small, clean hands. He took the badge and looked at it and said, "Seems to be in order. My name's Whitehall, by the way. What's yours, son?"

"Cook, attached to the homicide squad."

"Even in their houses people aren't safe any more," Whitehall said in the voice which seemed so much deeper than the man. He was a small man. "When I was young people were safe in their houses. How old do you think I am, Cook?"

"I don't know, sir," Cook said.

"Eighty-three," Whitehall said. "Old enough to be Liz's great-grandfather. Only I'm not. Had a stroke two years ago and likely to have another, whatever Doc Reynolds says. What do you want me to tell you, young Cook?"

"From here," Cook said, "you have a good view of Mrs. Singleton's house. Just whether you saw anything Sunday afternoon, Mr. Whitehall. Or —" he looked around the room. There was a low, wide bed in a corner. "Perhaps," Cook said, "you were resting? At — oh, around four-thirty, say?"

"Paralyzed," Whitehall said. "Not senile. Not much time to waste sleeping, if that's what you mean. Sit and watch the world go by. Not that much of it does in Point Street. Few years ago I'd watch it go by in Paris. In London. All over. Not always like this, young man. Lots to remember."

"I'm sure you have," Cook said, looking down at the very clean old man who, immobilized, seemed somehow frisky; who sounded cheerful with little reason for cheer. Momentarily, and with something like guilt, Tony Cook felt the strength and flexibility in his own long legs.

"About Sunday afternoon?" Cook said. "You were looking out your window?"

"After they'd brought me lunch," Whitehall said. "Yes. And I saw this kid run out of the house. Away from the cop on the beat. But cop yelled at him and the kid turned around and came back. Nice-looking kid. Seen him before once or twice. Going into Jenny's house through the basement."

"Jenny's?"

"What everybody called her. Oh, I'd met her a few times. Been over there once or twice when I was still getting around. Damned handsome woman, Jennifer Singleton was. Damned good actress."

"Yes," Cook said. "About when you were sitting by the window, Mr. Whitehall?"

"General Whitehall, come down to it," Whitehall said. "Retired a hell of a long time ago. Before you were born, could be. From about three o'clock, I suppose. Until perhaps six. At six they let me have a drink. And if

I've been a good boy, a cigar. No cigarettes. Bad for my lungs. I say what the hell difference does it make and nurse says, 'Now, General, we don't want to worry Doctor, do we?' Nothing I'd rather do, come down to it. As for Sunday, part of the time I was reading, you know. Ever read *The Guns of August*, Cook?"

"No," Cook said. "I never have, General."

"Probably seems as far away to you as the Trojan War," Whitehall said. "Good book. If Von Kluck hadn't turned east. But he did, didn't he?"

Cook was inclined to say, "If you say so, General." Instead he said, "Look up from your book from time to time?"

"Conscious of movement outside," General Whitehall said. "Corners of your eyes, call it. I've got good eyes still, young Cook. They've left me that. What am I supposed to have seen? Outside the Singleton house. You can't see into it. Look."

Cook did as he was told, through one of the tall windows. The equally tall and more numerous windows of the Singleton house were opaquely curtained. He turned back. Whitehall noiselessly, quickly, wheeled himself to the window and sat beside Cook.

"Not supposed to see," Cook said. "Anything you did see. A girl says she went into the house during the afternoon. Through the basement door. The boy may have let her in."

"No," Whitehall said. "I didn't see any girl. Which doesn't prove there wasn't one, does it? Pretty girl?"

"Yes," Cook said. "They say she's pretty. See anybody go into the house that way, General? A man, perhaps?"

"The boy," Whitehall said. "But that was a lot earlier. Middle of the day some time. Weekdays service people go in that way. Grocery boys and cleaner's boys and the like. Not much on Sundays. The boy was the only one I saw go in through the basement."

"Through the front door?"

"Go in or come out?"

"Either one, General."

"No. Except Mrs. Singleton herself, of course."

"When was that, General?"

Cook asked the question very gently, as if he might, speaking otherwise, frighten away an answer.

"Around four-thirty, at a guess. A little before, if Nurse Frittle was on time. Hell of a name for a nurse, isn't it? For anybody, come to that."

"On time?"

"Blood pressure every two hours. Not that they don't know what I'm going to die of. Due at four-thirty. Jenny came home about then. A few minutes before, if Frittle was on the dot. Usually is, you know."

"Mrs. Singleton, General?"

"Came in a cab," General Whitehall said. "Sixteen-thirty or about then."

"Alone? And went into the house?"

"Came alone, I'm pretty sure. But maybe the man came with her. Or maybe he'd just been waiting for her. I've a feeling that was it. Could be I'd seen him. Got a glimpse of him standing around in front of the house. Before the cab pulled up. Or, maybe, walking back and forth in front of it. Nothing I could swear to, Cook. But he did join her, if he wasn't in the cab with her."

"Yes?" Cook said, still in the gentle tone. If you reach out too quickly, too eagerly, you may frighten. Not that this sprightly old man seemed likely to frighten easily. "This man joined her?"

"The cab pulled up to the curb on her side," Whitehall said. "Had her money ready, at a guess. Women don't mostly. Didn't in my day. Had to scrummage around through these bags they carry. She was quick, as if she'd had her money out for a block or two. Got out and the cab pulled away and there this man was. Held out his hand to her and said something."

"She take his hand? As if he were a friend, I mean?"

"I think she did."

"Did they just stand there? As if they were a couple of acquaintances met by chance?"

"That I can't tell you," General Whitehall said. "Because then Frittle came in with this gadget of hers and said, 'Shall we turn ourselves around, General? For our light, you know.' Talk the damnedest way, don't they? So I turned my baby carriage around so the light would fall on her pressure gadget and she took my pressure."

"And?"

"I said, 'Do I win my cigar, Nurse?' Because it's always a secret between them and God or somebody. If it's higher than usual, I don't get the cigar. Got a match, Cook? Or a lighter?"

Cook got a lighter out of his pocket. And General Whitehall got a cigar out from under the white blanket. "Want to close the door for me, Cook?" Whitehall said. "She snoops."

Cook walked across the big room and closed the door. The girl named Elizabeth was on the stair landing outside, looking in. He closed the door on her, rather expecting her to block it with a foot. She did not. He went back to the scrubbed little old man and lighted his cigar. Whitehall drew on it gratefully. It smelled to Cook like a good cigar.

"This man," Cook said. "What did he look like?"

Whitehall blew fragrant smoke into the air and regarded it as it eddied there. But then he shook his head.

"Not very big," Whitehall said. "Of course, I was looking down on him, which can distort things like that. Had on a dark suit, I think. Oh, yes, he wore a hat. Pulled down over his forehead, I think. I can't give you much to go on, Cook."

Then he looked at Cook keenly through his bright blue eyes — his strangely youthful blue eyes.

"Thought it was this boy did it," Whitehall said. "Sounded like that on TV and the radio. In the *Times* even. Not that the *Times* said so. Well, Cook?"

"It may have been," Cook said. "We look a lot of places, General. It's possible this man may have gone into the house with her?"

"I suppose so. Possible, I mean. When Frittle finished and said, 'We'll see about the cigar, won't we, General?' and got the hell out, I wheeled around and looked out the window. No sign of Jenny. Or the man. She'd have had time to go into the house. He'd have had time to walk out of sight. Or go in with her."

"Dark suit," Cook said. "Hat. Dark hat, too?"

"Yes. All I can tell you about it."

"Not very big, you said. Any idea how tall, General?"

"No. As I said, I was looking down on him."

"Taller than Mrs. Singleton herself?"

"Yes. But she was not at all tall, Cook. Off-stage, I mean. On-stage — well, she was as tall as she wanted to be. They can do that, Cook. Add cubits to their stature. They say Edwin Booth did that. But he was before even my time, young Cook. As not much is any more. I —"

The door opened abruptly and a nurse, with the cap of her profession on the back of her head, came abruptly through it. From just inside the door she said, "*General. We're cheating!*" She looked at Cook and frowned at him. She looked, Cook thought, as if her name might well be Frittle.

"It is time," Nurse Frittle said, "for General Whitehall to have his rest. Whoever you are."

XI

Nathan Shapiro went down the staircase indicated to him and came to a long room with a bar across one end. There were cushioned benches along one wall leading from the bar, and a table with a round of cheese on it; there were chairs backing toward the rear of the room, where there was a pool table which two men were using. A man sat in one of several tall chairs set along the side of that part of the room and watched the players.

There were four men standing at the bar with glasses in their hands. They were talking; they paid no attention to the tall, sad-faced man who came — a little tentatively, since he did not belong there — into the barroom of The Players Club. Shapiro said, "Mr. Morton?" not raising his voice because, however preoccupied, a man will hear his own name.

The man who turned and looked at him and then said "Yes?" was a trim man and several inches under six feet. He wore a blue jacket with an insignia of some sort on the left breast.

He had black hair, recently and carefully cut. He had wide cheekbones and, below them, his face went down in clean planes to the bones of a cleanly outlined jaw. For a moment, Shapiro thought he had seen him somewhere before. He could not remember where, or of whom the man reminded him. Then he thought, "Gage," and, simultaneously, that he was wrong. This man did not look in the least like Gage. Except — Shapiro groped in his mind as Kurt Morton moved across the room to join him. He came up with the thought that both Kurt Morton and Joseph Gage had actor's faces. Which wasn't much to come up with. They both had decisive faces.

Morton, in the few steps he took toward Shapiro, moved lightly, like a young man. But he could not be really young, if he was the right Morton. His hair was very black and his wide-set eyes were black too.

He said, "Looking for me, Mr. —?"

"Shapiro," Shapiro told him. "Police lieutenant."

Morton said, "Oh," and his decisive voice went a little less decisive. He said, "You the man who called up a while back? Wanted to see me?"

"I called," Shapiro said.

Morton said, "Oh," again, in the diminished tone he had used before. He said, "Thought it might be somebody else. One producer keeps hounding me. I keep telling him I'm not interested in the part. However. What can I do for you, Lieutenant? About poor dear Jenny? Haven't seen her for a long time, Lieutenant. However."

He went toward the chairs at a round table and motioned, and Shapiro went after him. Morton still carried his drink. He sat down in one of the chairs and motioned toward another and said, "Buy you a drink, Lieutenant?"

Shapiro shook his head.

"You investigating poor dear Jenny's taking off?" Morton asked him. There was a slight British intonation in his voice. "Thought you people had your man for that, Lieutenant. One of these hippy kids, I thought it was."

"We have to go through a good deal of routine," Shapiro said. "You hadn't seen your former wife for some time, you say?"

"Oh," Morton said, "in this play she was doing. Flimsy bit, for my money. Agee's tapering off. May as well face it. But you didn't mean that, did you? Hadn't seen her, as *her* if you take me, for damn near a year. At a guess. Not exactly palsy, we haven't been. Since we split up. Make any difference, since this hippy kid killed her?"

"Cases like this," Shapiro said, "we find out

all we can about everybody. A lot of it, as you say, doesn't make any difference. Some years ago you and Mrs. Singleton separated. Probably don't know much about her life recently."

"What everybody knows," Morton said. He finished his drink and put the empty glass down and said, across the room, "I'm running dry, Joe."

The bartender said, "Right along, Mr. Morton."

"Married Agee," Kurt Morton said. "Then this twerp Gage. Still trying to be a juvenile, Gage-boy is. The lady got around, Lieutenant. That you have to say for Jenny. They say a lot of things, but that you've got to say."

"What things, Mr. Morton?"

"From the way some of them talk," Morton said, "You'd think she was Bernhardt and Duse and Hayes all rolled into one. With a bit of Cornell and maybe Bankhead worked in. Queen of the American stage. Actually heard her called that."

"She wasn't all these — er — things?"

"Oh," Morton said, "part of the time she was good. When we were playing together she was sometimes pretty damn good. Not good comedy timing. I had to watch that. Play around it. Set the timing for her. But she could laugh herself out of almost anything. That I'll give her."

The bartender brought Morton's new drink to the table. It wasn't, Shapiro thought, Morton's second drink of the day, which was still an immature day. Or, possibly, his third.

"You and Mrs. Singleton were a very famous team for some time, I understand," Shapiro said. "I don't know much about the theater, but I've heard that."

"You're damned right we were," Morton said. "Until — all right, until she got jealous."

Shapiro repeated the word.

"Oh," Morton said. "Professionally. Because there wasn't any hiding it. So, I'm a conceited so-and-so. But for years I carried her and she knew it and when she figured she had it made she got so she didn't like it."

"She seems to have done well enough after you and she split up," Shapiro said. "In a good many plays, from what I hear. Starred in a good many. That's right, isn't it?"

"Momentum," Morton said. "I taught her a lot. Gave her a push, you might say. And she kept rolling along. Happens that way, sometimes. No telling what audiences will go for. And she did have that laugh. I don't deny her that. And quite a few tricks, some of which we worked out together for her. And she had the looks. I don't deny her that, either."

"But," Shapiro said, "that she was a great actress. You do deny her that, Mr. Morton.

Anyway, it sounds as if you did."

"No evil of the dead," Morton said. "That's what they say, isn't it? So — sure, Lieutenant, she was a great actress. And a lovely woman who didn't look half her age. And the soul of generosity." He drank deeply. "When there was something in it for her," he said. Then he said, "Wash that last out, Lieutenant. Don't want to give you ideas."

"After you and she quit acting together," Shapiro said, "you kept on acting, I understand. Except, recently, not so often, somebody told me."

"When something comes along that I fall for," Morton said. "Can afford to pick and choose, you know. Not take anything that somebody wants me for. Lot of trashy stuff around now. Things I wouldn't touch. Not like Jenny. Anything she could do that gurgle in was good enough for Jenny."

"Gurgle?"

"All right, gurgling laughter."

"Recently," Shapiro said, "I understand you haven't found many plays you thought were worth appearing in? Many that, as you say, you fell for?"

"Not for a season or two," Morton said. "Have to keep my standards up, if you know what I mean."

"But when you and Mrs. Singleton were acting together — famous together, way I understand it — you appeared in a good many plays. More good plays available in those days?"

"We were a team," Morton said. "Writers tailored plays for us. Plays with two good leads. Those days, you got the Mortons to sign and you pretty much had it made. If you wrote plays, or produced them. Mostly Les Agee wrote our plays. Pretty good he was, in those days."

Morton drank from his glass.

"You getting anywhere with all this?" he asked Shapiro. "Ancient history, I'd think. I suppose you know your business, but I'd think we were getting rather far afield."

"Just background," Shapiro told him. "Hard to tell sometimes what may turn out to be pertinent. Just trying to get the picture, Mr. Morton. From different angles, call it. For example, what you say about Mrs. Singleton as an actress is a bit different from what other people have told us."

"I acted with her," Morton said. "Worked things out with her. And was married to her."

"Sure," Shapiro said. "Speaking of the marriage, Mr. Morton. Which of you decided to end it?"

"Any of your business?"

"Probably not. You don't need to tell me

if you don't want to, Mr. Morton. I would rather like to know."

"Call it mutual," Morton said. "Mutual agreement to disagree."

"Whatever you say," Shapiro said. "She didn't, say, fall in love with Agee and walk out on you?"

"Nothing like that. Oh, she did marry Agee. Sure. On the rebound."

"And Agee went on writing plays for her," Shapiro said. "The way you say he did for both of you as a team."

"Yes."

"Not plays with parts in them for you?"

"Nothing I'd touch. I told you he's gone off in recent years."

"Yes," Shapiro said. "I know you told me that, Mr. Morton. And that you're choosy about the plays you appear in. This producer you thought might have been the one telephoned you today. After you to appear in a play, you said. A play, you think, you might like to appear in?"

"Haven't read it," Morton said. "He wants me to. So how do I know? And, what are you getting around to, anyway?"

"Just trying to get the picture," Shapiro said. "Were you in a play last season, Mr. Morton?"

"No. Had plenty of offers, but as I told you —"

"Yes," Shapiro said. "How about the season before last?"

"Well, they decided not to bring that one in. Didn't jell. And the director and Jamey managed to louse it up between them."

"Jamey?"

"James Bouton. He had the lead. And upstaged everybody, like always."

"What kind of part did you have, Mr. Morton?"

"Good part. One a real actor could get his teeth into. Not the biggest in the show. I don't say that. But one I could feel my way into."

Shapiro said he saw, which was not entirely true. He said, "Since you and Mrs. Singleton — Mrs. Morton then, of course — split up, how many plays have you had parts in, Mr. Morton? Or would you rather I'd look it up?"

Morton leaned forward across the table. He brushed his almost empty glass so that it teetered, but he caught it before it fell. He said, "I've had about enough of this. This prying into what's none of your goddamn business."

"All right," Shapiro said. "Does for an answer, doesn't it? Something that is my business, Mr. Morton. Mind telling me where you were Sunday evening? Around five, say?"

"So that's it," Morton said. "After all this beating about the bush."

"Part of it," Shapiro said. "Always part of it. Well? Here?"

"Where I wasn't," Morton said, "was at Jenny's house killing her."

"Where you were?"

"Had lunch here. Went up to my room afterward for a siesta. Get sleepy after lunch."

"In your room from about when to about when?"

"Three-thirty. Maybe four. Until about six. Want to know what I did after that?"

"Not particularly," Shapiro said.

"Open-house night," Morton said. "Let the ladies in then. Dozens of people can tell you where Kurt Morton was then."

"I don't doubt it," Shapiro said. "Don't doubt it at all. You expect to stay here at the club for long, Mr. Morton?"

"Any of your business?"

"Oh," Shapiro said, "cases like this we like to know where people are likely to be."

He left it there and climbed the stairs out of the barroom. He had the feeling that Morton was staring at him as he went up the stairs, and that there would be dislike, even bitterness, in Morton's black eyes.

Morton was, Shapiro thought, as he walked in search of a sidewalk telephone booth, a bitter man. Conceivably, he was a man who had brooded over the collapse of a career which had once been shining. Brooded and blamed? Felt bitterness?

That, as he walked away from Gramercy Park, seemed possible to Lieutenant Nathan Shapiro. But that it was enough did not seem very likely.

Of course, Shapiro thought, as he shut the door of a telephone booth behind him, I don't know anything about people like these. Don't know what they are capable of. As usual, I'm the wrong man for the job.

Mrs. Raymond Franklin was not at home. She was at a luncheon of the Village Preservation Association. She probably would be home early because it was her day to have the discussion group and the group's time was three. About two-thirty, she'd be home, probably. Not later or much later. Yes, she would be told that Lieutenant — what was the name again? — Lieutenant Shapiro would like to talk to her for a few minutes. And that he would like her to call him back to fix a time when she might be free. At?

Shapiro gave the number, and repeated it while she — unidentified, except that she had said "Mrs. Franklin's residence" with a maid's rising inflection — wrote the number down.

Shapiro had a hot dog at a counter and a cup of tea to wash it down. He was finishing the tea and having a cigarette with it when something occurred to him. It was only a glimmer of a something. He found another telephone box and a Manhattan telephone directory and Temple Productions, with an address in the Forties. He spun another dial.

Who wished to speak to Mr. Temple? Oh, police business. Probably Mr. Temple was out to lunch. If — what was the name again? — would wait a moment she would ring his office. Possibly his secretary —

A man said, "Temple." Then he said, "Same detective was here yesterday? Told him all I had to tell."

"No," Shapiro said, "not Detective Cook, Mr. Temple," and said who it was and said he would like a few minutes of Mr. Temple's time.

"Tomorrow," Temple said. "I'm just going to lunch. And I'm tied up for the rest of the day. See you tomorrow about —"

"Perhaps," Shapiro said, "we can clear a small point up on the telephone. Not more than five minutes."

Temple said, "Shoot. And make it short."

"About an actor named Kurt Morton," Shapiro said. "Used to be married to Mrs. Singleton. Acted together and —"

"For God's sake, man," Temple said. "I know all that. Produced their plays. So what about Morton?"

"Is he a good actor?"

"Yes. Used to be damn good sometimes."

"He hasn't acted much lately?"

"No."

"Why?"

"Hard to say precisely. People got to thinking of him as part of a team. No team, couldn't visualize him alone. Not at his salary, anyway."

"You yourself, Mr. Temple?"

Temple said he didn't get it.

"Haven't had a — script, that's the word, isn't it — with a part in it for Mr. Morton? One you thought of producing. Perhaps even talked to him about?"

It was, Temple said, funny he should ask that. Shapiro waited to be told why it was funny.

"Les Agee's working on a script now," Temple said. "Rough at the moment. But I've got an option on it. I was thinking of putting it on with Jenny starred after *Always Good-bye* finished. Down the drain that is, now, of course. It's got a part in it that'd be right for Kurt. If I decide to do it when Les gets through fiddling with it, and if I can get somebody who can do the Jennifer Singleton role, I may give him a shot at it."

"With an actress not Mrs. Singleton," Shapiro said. "Not if she hadn't been killed? I mean, not with Morton in it?"

"Oh," Temple said, "I thought of that. Would have had some publicity value. The 'together again' sort of bilge. Not that they'd have been a team again. Part I had in mind for Kurt isn't a lead part. Don't know, actually, whether he'd have taken it with Jenny starred, on his uppers as he probably is."

"You talked to him about it?"

"No. Did talk to Jenny, poor darling. Showed her part of Les's rough. Wanted her part built up, of course. Like they all do."

"Did you mention the chance you might hire Morton for apart in this play?"

"Sounded her out," Temple said. "She nixed it. Good and hard she nixed it. Said I must be out of my ever-loving. Said didn't I know Kurt was a has-been? Said if Kurt was going to be in the show I'd have to get me another girl."

"Which you weren't going to do?"

"To be in my business," Temple said, "you've got to be a little crazy, Lieutenant. But you don't have to be that crazy. You don't trade a Jennifer Singleton for a Kurt Morton. Look — people I'm having lunch with are *backers*. Backers, man!"

"Just one more thing," Shapiro said. "Would Mr. Morton have known his former wife had, as you say, nixed him for this role?"

"He might have, I suppose. Jenny, poor darling, was pretty steamed up. She may have talked about it. And things, God knows, get around in the profession."

"With Mrs. Singleton out of the picture, he might get this part if you put on the play Mr. Agee is working on?"

"If I go on with it. Find somebody for Jenny's role. Yes, I may give him a shot at it. And now, for God's sake, I've —"

"Yes, Mr. Temple. Thanks for your time."

Tony Cook called in. Lieutenant Shapiro was out somewhere. Cook went in and typed a report, with carbons, about his interview with General (Ret.) Whitehall. What had for a few minutes seemed important seemed to shrivel in typescript. Mrs. Jennifer Singleton had, half an hour or so before she was killed, met a small man as she got out of a taxi in front of her house. Had, perhaps, talked to him for a minute or two. No useful description of the man, except that he wasn't big and wore a dark suit and a hat. A neighbor who was also an acquaintance, out for a stroll on a pleasant Sunday afternoon. Hundred to one he had said good afternoon to an acquaintance and continued his stroll.

Cook had lunch and went to Centre Street and talked a face to a man with a pencil. As he talked, by slow degrees, the moving pencil traced the face. "About so?" "Not quite so heavy." That was of a jaw. "Like this?" "A bit higher, maybe." That was of a left eyebrow. "Doesn't show that much with his chin down." That was about a scar. When no photograph is available, and the face Cook talked was not in the mug file, special members of the New York Police Department who have ready pencils put bits and pieces together and come up with faces. "He had a square sort of face," one witness says. "His hair bushed out at the sides." The trouble is, of course, that people usually don't look much at other people — don't really look.

Tony Cook was a professional and one with a memory for faces. As he talked the face he wanted, he used a pencil of his own. "Something like this," he said of an ear, and made lines which were something, if not much, like the lines of a human ear. The sketch artist, a sergeant, put an ear on the face which was slowly taking form. He said, "About like that?" "Pretty much," Tony Cook said.

It was done, finally. "Yes," Tony Cook said, "that's pretty much our baby."

Copies were made for distribution. Tony took one of them and went to work Sixth Avenue, which seemed the mostly likely street to work. Not that there weren't, probably, thousands of places all over the city where keys were duplicated. Sixth Avenue would be handiest for a man who lived on Morton Street.

It isn't exciting to go from store to store and show a sketch of a man's face and say, "Ever see this man around? Did he ever come in to have a key made? Copied?" Most of the things a policeman has to do aren't particularly exciting, and nothing comes of most of them. For the most part, policemen just trudge along.

(And once a good many policemen trudged from shop to shop, then too on Sixth Avenue, and showed storekeepers what was not even the sketch of a face — which was a chalk mark somebody had neglected to rub off a trunk which had a fresh body in it. And, four hours or so after the trunk, which had begun to leak blood, was left on an express company's dock, they had the man who had bought a trunk from a shop on Sixth Avenue and put a body in it. Considerately, he had had the trunk delivered to a flat he had shared with the man he had decided would be better off dead.)

Tony Cook trudged up the west side of Sixth Avenue and showed his sketch and asked his question. He got, "Sorry. Doesn't ring any bell with me." He got, "Man who cuts keys for us is off today." He got, "Every day we get maybe a dozen people who want keys copied," and then what was not quite a leer. "Girls want 'em for their boy friends. And the other way around. You know how it is."

Cook said he knew how it was and went on up the block and into another place with a sign, "Keys Made." There was only one man in this store and Cook waited while he went, at the behest of a young woman in a very mini-skirt, to find something he thought he had somewhere. He came back, after a lapse of time, with a can of paint. "Gloss," the young woman said. "Not what I want at *all*. I told you gloss wouldn't do *at* all."

The man, after he had shrugged and sighed and returned the rejected can of paint to a rear room, looked at the sketch Cook showed him. He looked at it with greater care than the others had; he carried it to the front of the store where the light was better.

He said, "I don't know. Seems like I've seen him somewhere around. Don't remember it was about a key. Seen him on the street around here, seems like. Or — hold it a minute."

Cook held it a minute.

"Got it," the man said. "Maybe I've got it anyway. Man looks like that, sort of, works in the Ace Market. Waits on trade. Now and then I pick up things there for the missus. Or go in with her to pinch avocados. Know what I mean?"

"Pinch?" Cook said and then, "Oh, sure. Girl I know pinches them. This man works there, you think? Happen to know what his name is?"

"Seems like they call him Ralph. All I know about him."

"But he hasn't been in to have a key made?"

"Not that I remember. Could be when Benny's around. Happens Benny's out making a delivery right now. But mostly I make the keys myself. Benny sometimes picks the wrong blanks. And they won't fit in. Know what I mean?"

Anyway, Tony Cook thought as he walked on toward Fourteenth Street, we came up with something, Sergeant Strothers and I. We came up with a face which looks something, anyway, like Ralph Baker's face. There's that.

He crossed Sixth Avenue and worked down the other side. Nobody recognized the face he showed as that of a man who had had a Yale key copied within recent weeks. Perhaps somebody else would have better luck somewhere else. There were a good many copies of the sketch in a good many hands by now. And, of course, if Baker had had his son's key to the Singleton house copied with intent to use it for burglary, he might have been smart enough to have the copy made where he wasn't known.

At around four in the afternoon, Cook knocked it off for the day and checked in, and out, at Homicide, Manhattan South. Shapiro was not there. Cook added to his report the unimportant fact that nobody on Sixth Avenue from West Fourth Street to Fourteenth Street could positively identify a sketch of Ralph Baker, father of a boy who had found a body. Who said he had found a body.

XII

Mrs. Raymond Franklin was, Shapiro thought, in her early forties. She was trim and quick and looked a good deal like her daughter. Of course she wanted to help. And she thought it wise, very wise, of the police not to be too easily satisfied. It was then almost five in the afternoon, because Mrs. Franklin had not got home until a few minutes before three and she'd had people coming in. Because if they ever do get around to tearing that awful thing down they ought to make a park there, not another apartment house, which probably would be just as out of character as the jail. And the library ought to have a park to go with it. And couldn't she give Lieutenant Shapiro something? Because she was going to have a sherry herself.

They were in a big living room by then and Shapiro was, as he usually was, trying to catch up. Mrs. Raymond Franklin was unquestionably brisk. And decisive. Shapiro did, as he refused a drink, identify the jail which might be torn down as the House of Detention for Women and the library as the former Jefferson Market Court House. Rose had been very pleased when the courthouse had been turned into a library, after having been for years merely a contorted hulk. It was only a few blocks from Clayton High School and thus convenient for any students who might be interested in reading books.

Why had Mrs. Franklin put up bail for Roy Baker?

"Because he's a nice clean boy and it's all an awful mistake."

"You speak," Shapiro said, "as if you know the boy, Mrs. Franklin. Do you?"

"Not actually. But my daughter does. And she's told me about him and she's a — a perceptive child."

"Since he was held as a material witness? I mean had she talked about Roy before that? She seems to feel strongly about him."

"Well, no. Oh, I thought there was, recently, some special boy. But I don't pry, Lieutenant. I want my daughter — both Ray and I want our daughter — to feel that we have *confidence* in her. And to feel that she can come to us, tell us things, only when she wants to. Because we trust her. And want her to know we trust her. Do you have any children,

Lieutenant Shapiro?"

"No."

"But you are married?"

"Yes," Shapiro said. "I'm married. To get back to —"

"*Lieutenant,*" Mrs. Franklin said. "I know your name isn't an uncommon one, of course. But by any chance is your wife the assistant principal at Clayton High?"

"Yes," Shapiro said. "You put up the bond money for young Baker because your daughter — well, likes him? Just like that?"

"I suppose it comes to that, really. But — he couldn't have been the one who killed poor Mrs. Singleton. And so he shouldn't be locked up. Kept locked up. Just because he's a poor boy. Gangsters and people like that can always put up bail money, can't they? And it isn't fair, is it?"

"No," Shapiro said. "I don't suppose it's fair. It's just the way things are."

"They oughtn't to be," Mrs. Franklin said. She said it firmly; she was, Shapiro thought, a very firm woman.

"Did your husband approve of your putting up bail for young Baker?"

"Actually, I didn't bother him about it. Just wrote a check and had it certified, because they said they wanted that, and had Stella — she's my secretary — run down with it. And they've let the boy go, haven't they?"

"Yes. They've let the boy go. You do believe your daughter was with him Sunday afternoon? And, went upstairs with him and that Mrs. Singleton was dead, or dying, by the time they found her?"

"Of course," Mrs. Franklin said. "Of course I do. Ellen doesn't tell untruths, Lieutenant. You think I don't know my own daughter?"

There was, Shapiro decided, no point in going into that with this firm woman. There had, probably, been little point in coming to see her at all. She was loyal to her daughter's loyalty; loyal to the extent of five thousand dollars. That was all there was to it. And, at a guess, five thousand wasn't much of anything to the Franklins. So —

"Sorry to have bothered you," Shapiro said. "Taken up your time this way. We just have to —"

He didn't finish, because a maid in a blue uniform came in, carrying a telephone which was not attached to anything.

"There's a call for Lieutenant Shapiro, ma'am," the maid said. "Shall I plug it in?"

"Of course," Mrs. Franklin said. "It doesn't work if you don't plug it in, Lucile," and then, to Shapiro, "Somebody knew you'd be here?"

"Pretty much a rule," Shapiro said. "They always want to know." He took the telephone

226

from the maid after she had plugged it and said his name into it. He listened and said "O.K., I'll get along up there." He listened again. "Oh, yes," he said. "We'll have to, of course. It could have been that way. Get Cook on it."

He put the telephone down on a table. Mrs. Franklin was looking at him, firmly and with her eyebrows arched.

"A man we're interested in has met with an accident," Shapiro said.

Tony Cook went uptown by subway and walked some blocks west and climbed two flights of stairs and let himself into his small apartment, which was as closely hot as he had expected it to be. He opened what windows it had and thought, as he usually thought, that it was time he moved downtown. This West Bronx place had been all right when he was assigned to a precinct squad nearby. It was one hell of a long way from West Twentieth Street and Homicide South. It was, of course, even farther from an apartment in Gay Street and the girl who lived in it.

Tony Cook shaved, although he had shaved that morning. He showered. He put on slacks and a summer jacket and looked at himself. Too gay, the jacket? Too much a jacket for the country? He changed to a light gray summer suit. The suit jacket buttoned more smoothly over the handgun in its shoulder holster.

It was almost five-thirty by then, and he wasn't due for an hour. She had got used to his being punctual but had, a few months ago, implied, without flatly saying, that punctuality could be carried too far. "Mister," Rachel Farmer had said, "You ought to give a girl time to dress." She had said that with her apartment door opened just enough so that she could look out around it. She had unhooked the safety chain, but by the time he got in she was across the room, walking away from him with that long stride of hers. She hadn't, certainly, had time to dress.

When he first met Rachel Farmer she hadn't, apparently, cared whether she had clothes on or not or even, Tony had sometimes thought, known whether she had or hadn't. She had been in sweater and slacks when he first saw her and was in the process of stealing a drawing, which she insisted was of herself, from the studio of a painter who had just been murdered. She had been very tall and thin in sweater and slacks and had moved, Tony thought then, rather like a man.

When he next saw her she was, unconcernedly, not wearing anything at all and Tony had noticed, sharply, that she was not in the least like a man. And when, off duty, he had first gone around to take her out to dinner, she had been wearing a sleek white dress with a red belt around her slim waist and white shoes with heels which made her even taller than she really was. She had, that evening, been quite a surprise to Tony Cook.

She still was, Tony thought, sipping a short drink with his feet up and waiting until it was time to go downtown again. She kept on being. She still now and then called him "mister," but she called "mister" anybody the term suited, or almost suited. Its suitability, among the Village people she knew and he was getting to know, was rather often a tossup.

He looked at his watch often while he killed time and a small drink. Not too punctual, he told himself. But not too late, either. Sometimes you had to wait a while for a downtown express.

At around six he went down the two flights to the hot street and walked toward the subway station. As he closed the street door he heard a telephone ringing behind him, but he decided it wasn't his. She wouldn't be calling up to break their date. She didn't break their dates.

At Fourteenth Street he changed to a local and had to wait several minutes for it. He walked with long strides the few blocks from the West Fourth Street station to Gay Street, and he was on the dot. He waited a few moments for the dot to pass before he pressed a doorbell. Not that he would fool her any. She knew he was eager. He sometimes thought she knew almost everything there was to know about him. The lock release chattered at him and he went up a flight of stairs. Her door was opening when he reached the top of the flight.

She wasn't wearing the white dress this time. She was wearing a pale green dress. She had, he thought, recently had her black hair done. She said, "Hullo, mister." He didn't kiss her because she had, obviously, just put lipstick on and, anyway, they didn't kiss much except when it wasn't casual. He did put an arm around her and hold her close against him for a moment and then patted her tenderly on the fanny. She was wearing a panty girdle which she didn't need. She'd certainly changed a lot since he first met her and thought maybe she had killed a man.

She had ice out where it usually was and his bourbon and a little pitcher of water and a glass for bourbon and water. He knew his way, and took it, to the refrigerator, where she kept La Ina and the glass chilling for it, and he poured for them both while she sat on a sofa with her knees together but, because it was a year for short skirts, pleasantly visible. He sat beside her and they touched glasses.

"I," Rachel Farmer said, "am being immortalized. Don't you think that's nice, Tony?"

"Fine," he said.

"With clothes on, for once," Rachel said. "Some, anyway. And sitting down, if you'll believe it. By Rafe Lorenson. The 'Rafe' is for 'Raphael,' or he thinks it is. It's a portrait and I'll be immortal. A hundred years from now they'll be debating who his model was. Which will make the immortality a little wispy, won't it? So I told him I'd take the cash and let the credit go, if it was all the same."

Rachel Farmer was a model. She posed for painters and photographers. Her nonchalance about nakedness was a professional, acquired characteristic.

But for Tony she dressed most carefully, even to the point of a panty girdle to which stockings could be hitched. Which was gratifying, in a puzzling sort of way. It made her sometimes nakedness for him a special thing — a selected gift. She said, now, "Are you listening, mister? Because you look as if you weren't. Or don't you like the dress?"

"Very much," he said. "You are going to be immortalized by a painter named Rafe. And he lets you pose sitting down."

"With clothes on, even," she said. "Head and shoulders. Well, mostly shoulders, come down to it. Actually, somewhat more. And what have you been doing, Tony? By the way, your gun's showing. Usually you remember to take it off."

Tony Cook stood up and took his jacket off and his gun off. When they went out to dinner he would, of course, have to put it back on again. It was the light gun he could wear, legally, when he was off duty.

"It was a cruel thing about Jennifer Singleton," Rachel said. "A mad thing. For a few dollars." She sipped her drink and looked at nothing. "Years ago. When I was young," Rachel Farmer said, "I saw her for the first time. I've forgotten what she was in. Somehow the plays she was in never seemed to matter much. I decided I'd be an actress, like her. Did I ever tell you I wanted to be an actress, Tony?"

"No," Tony said.

"Of course," Rachel said, "I've wanted to be a lot of things, really. One thing one day, and another thing another. When I was young, of course."

"You're young," Tony said.

"Not in the same way," she said. "After I saw her the first time I used to walk by that house of hers, even when I was really going another way, or should have been. I thought, she'll come out sometime and see me and say, 'You ought to be on the stage, young woman.' Or, perhaps, 'My dear.' It was when I was seventeen or eighteen. And already I was too tall, of course. I didn't know it yet. On the stage, women can't be as tall as men, you know. And most men aren't taller than I am."

"You want to measure, lady?"

"Not fair," Rachel said. "I've got heels on."

"We could, of course —"

He was told to drink his drink and then, gently, laughed at. He shrugged an inquiry.

"Your eyes, Tony. I've learned about your eyes. Drink your drink and we'll have another and go out to dinner. I don't say we won't see who's the taller, darling. Later. Are you working — you and Mr. Shapiro — on the Singleton thing? Or is it, as it sounds in the newspapers, all solved?"

It had looked like being, he told her. Now they weren't so sure.

"I don't suppose," he said, "she ever did come out when you were walking by her house?"

"Never."

"You never did meet her? I mean — the Village is a neighborhood, in its special sort of way. More than most places in Manhattan.

She lived only a few blocks from here. And, there are circles down here."

"Concentric," Rachel said. "Perhaps overlapping is what I mean, not concentric."

"People interested in the same things," Cook said. "In — I suppose it's called the arts."

"Not by me, mister. Not ever by me."

"You know what I mean, Rachel. Maybe I use the wrong words. After all, I'm a cop, think like a cop, I guess."

"Being a cop's all right," Rachel said. "Did you ever want to be something else? A doctor? Or — I don't know. A professor. The president of something? The way I wanted to be an actress?"

"I tried to get into Annapolis once," Cook said. "Or, I guess, just thought of trying. Nothing came of it. And once I wanted to be a cowboy. When I was about twelve, probably. Being a cop's all right."

"I just said that," Rachel said. "Yes, I do know people around here. All sorts of people. People who want to go on the stage. And one or two who are on it. And two men who want to write plays. And a woman who's been writing a novel for years and years. One of the things I wanted to be years ago, when I was young, was a poet. Because it doesn't matter how tall poets are. It's how tall their words are."

He held his glass out and, after a moment during which she merely looked at him, she held hers to click with his.

"Circles touching circles," he said. "Within circles. Jennifer Singleton in any of them?"

"She was much older than the people I know," Rachel said. "I don't think —" she stopped at that and looked at her almost empty sherry glass as if a thought might be dissolved in it.

"One of the boys who're trying to write plays," she said, "told me once he knew Mrs. Singleton. We were talking about the theater, which is all he ever talks about. He — I'm trying to remember, although I don't see that it matters. Oh, yes — that he'd met her some place and sent her a play of his to read. Because he thought there was a character in it she might be interested in creating. That was the word he used."

"Did she read it?"

"He said she did. And that she was very sweet and encouraging about it. But — I remember now — that the part he had thought of for her should be played by an older woman. Which, he said, made him wonder if she'd really read the script. Because the character he'd had in mind for her was about forty-five. And she, Tony?"

"Late fifties," he said. "Almost sixty. And

not looking it by years. I didn't know people who wrote plays sent them to actors. I'd have thought they'd send them to producers."

"I don't know," she said. "This one says he did. And it seems to me I've heard about people sending scripts to movie stars. It's not anything I know about. I stand up, usually in cold places with nothing on, and people paint pictures of me. Of what they see when they look at me, anyway. Remember the one Briskie did of me with two heads?"

"Yes," Cook said and looked at her carefully. "One head," he said, "is better than two." He looked at her empty glass and at his own. "And two drinks than one," he said. He arranged that.

They talked after that about things of no consequence except to them. For their second drink he sat beside her on the sofa. He looked down at her feet. "I don't," he said, "see how women stand up on such high heels. I'd think they'd teeter. But you don't."

She turned and looked at him and smiled at him.

"All this about being tall," Tony said. "Too tall to be an actress because men have to be —"

She patted his knee. Then she stood up.

"Tony," Rachel said, "I think we'd better go to dinner."

He stood, too. He said, "Charles?"

"Nick's, I'd rather," she said. "Because I feel like pasta. Do you feel like pasta?"

He said that pasta would be fine.

"At Nick's," Rachel said, "Lasagna and things like that just have to be dished up."

Tony Cook put his gun on and they went down the stairs to Gay Street. As he was closing the outside door after them a telephone, muted, rang somewhere in the house.

"It could be mine," Rachel said. "But it would stop before we could get back, wouldn't it?"

They walked away through crooked Gay Street.

Nick Gazzi's restaurant was not crowded, and Nick, beaming at them — Nick approved of them — served lasagna quickly and each had a glass of chianti and, afterward, espresso. And they went back early to the apartment in Gay Street and sat side by side on the sofa and sipped very small glasses of cognac. And when the cognac was finished, Rachel pushed her left shoe off with the toes of her right foot and then the right shoe with her left.

"Now," she said, "you can be taller than she is. Wasn't that once an advertising slogan or something?"

Tony Cook did not answer that. He stood and pulled the tall girl to her stocking feet and held her against him. He was, by a very little, the taller.

"It still isn't fair," Rachel said. "There are heels on your shoes too."

"Above all," Tony said, "we must be fair."

They went together into the bedroom.

Lying side by side on the bed they were both long people. They lined naked feet up to a chalk line they made believe was there, and she reached an arm up over her own head, the forearm straight. Her fingers touched his head an inch or two above his right ear.

"I guess so," Rachel said. "Maybe two inches taller. If you'd just lie still I could —"

He did not lie still.

"Be more exact," Rachel Farmer said. "But I guess it really doesn't —"

She did not finish that.

They were lying quietly again when the telephone rang. It seemed to them both to ring very loudly. It was on her side of the wide bed, and she reached out a long bare arm and lifted the receiver. She said, "Yes?" very softly. She listened for a moment and covered the mouthpiece with her hand and said, in a whisper this time, "Are you here?" to Tony Cook.

He raised his eyebrows.

She did not speak this time but formed a name with lip movements. He nodded his head.

238

"Yes, he is," Rachel said and then raised her voice and called, "Tony?" as if he were some distance away. He waited seconds and then reached across her and took the handset she held toward him. He said, "Yes, Lieutenant?"

"Been trying to get you all evening," Shapiro said. His voice rasped sadly. "Your apartment, Miss Farmer's. That Charles Restaurant you two go to. Where were you?"

There seemed to be no point in being too specific about that. "We didn't go to Charles tonight," Cook said.

He listened, then. He said, "I'll check it out, Nate," and reached the telephone back to Rachel, who put it in its cradle. Cook swung long legs out of the bed. She put a light on so he could find his clothes.

"Man named Agee," Tony said, stepping into shorts. "Fell in his apartment and banged his head on an andiron in the fireplace. Only maybe it wasn't that way. Maybe the andiron or something hit him. Any idea what I did with my shoes?"

"Probably under the bed," Rachel said. "But your gun's in the living room, I'm almost sure. It was the first thing you took off when we came back."

She turned on her side and watched him put on shirt and trousers.

"Lipstick came off on you," Rachel said. "They claim it's indelible, but it always does, doesn't it?"

"You're beautiful," Tony Cook said, and took the tissue she handed him and rubbed his lips with it.

He leaned down and kissed her, not on her lips because his now were clean of lipstick. He put his gun on and his jacket over it and went down a flight of stairs and, with long strides, through the Village streets to ask a boy where he had been when a man got hit on the back of the head, probably with a poker.

The man couldn't tell what he had been hit with. It was, according to the hospital, touch and go whether he'd ever tell anything again about anything.

XIII

Nathan Shapiro was not as late as he so often found himself to be. Two men from the precinct squad were there when he got to Lester Agee's apartment, and Arnold Mimms, Mr. Agee's man, had only told his story once. He told it again to Shapiro. He had a small, dry voice. He was a small, dry man. He had found Agee lying unconscious on the floor, his head against the uptilted end of a firedog in the empty fireplace. This had been at a little before five in the afternoon. He had come into the living room to get the ice container to take it to the kitchen to fill it. He did that every evening about that time. He had not expected Mr. Agee to be in the room.

"Mr. Agee has a regular schedule," Mimms told Shapiro and the two precinct men. "I serve him lunch at one. Then he goes to his office upstairs and works until, usually, about four-thirty. Then he showers and changes for the evening. I make sure that the things he may need are ready here when he has dressed."

"Here" was the big living room of the big duplex apartment — the room with a wall of glass at one end and, far below it, the East River. Mimms wore a white jacket and black trousers and stood thinly erect as he told his story.

He had come in through a door at the rear of the living room and had gone to the bar and picked up the ice container. There had been some ice still in it, but not enough. Also it had begun to melt. "Mr. Agee does not like slushy ice."

He had turned away from the bar, carrying the ice bucket, and only by chance had looked up the long room.

He had seen his employer's feet, sticking out from behind that chair. He pointed to the chair, which was one of those beside the fireplace.

"It was most peculiar," Mimms said. "I was quite concerned."

He had called his employer's name and got no answer. He had hurried up the room, saying, "Mr. Agee, sir. Mr. *Agee*."

He had found Agee lying on his back, his head against the firedog. His hair was matted with blood and there was blood on the end of the firedog.

"He was breathing very strangely," Mimms said. "He was unconscious. So I called Dr.

242

Rolfe. Then I lifted his head enough to put a pillow under it. The doctor came almost at once. His office is downstairs."

"It didn't occur to you to call the police, Mr. Mimms?" Shapiro asked him.

"I assumed he had fallen and hit his head," Mimms said. "I did not think it a matter for the police."

Dr. Rolfe, after a brief examination, had used the telephone — used it to call an ambulance, to arrange for a hospital room and, last, to call the police emergency number. They had not had to wait long. The doctor had ridden with Lester Agee in the ambulance.

"The doctor seem to agree with you that it was an accident? That Mr. Agee had fallen and struck his head on the firedog?"

"He didn't say."

"But he did call the police." Shapiro turned to one of the precinct men. He said, "Anybody get in touch with this doctor?"

"At the hospital, his office says. Got a man there. Only he's still in the emergency ward with Agee. Seems, from what we can get at the hospital, that Agee's pretty bad."

Shapiro nodded. He turned back to Mimms. He said, "Mr. Agee have dizzy spells that you know of? Anything like that?"

"No. Not that I know of."

"Does he drink much? Enough to make him

unsteady on his feet?"

"I've never seen him unsteady, Lieutenant. He is a most moderate man."

"Did he have any visitors this afternoon?"

About that Mimms could not be certain. He had himself gone out after three and been gone for perhaps an hour. There had been "certain errands." He had gone into the apartment through the service door and back to his own quarters, which were beyond the kitchen.

"Down at the desk," one of the precinct men said, "they say nobody got announced to Agee. But that if somebody knew the apartment number they could just get into an elevator and go up, although they were supposed to stop at the desk first."

After Mimms had completed his errands and returned to the apartment he had not heard anything to make him think his employer had a guest. He had heard no voices. But he would not, from his own quarters beyond the kitchen, have been likely to hear anything from the living room or from Agee's office on the floor above. Sometimes, if Mr. Agee happened to leave his office door open, Mimms could hear his employer's typewriter. He did not remember hearing it that day. If, after he got back, somebody had rung the doorbell, Mimms would have heard it ring and would have gone to the door. The doorbell had not rung. Yes, Mr. Agee had known that Mimms had errands to do. Yes, if Mr. Agee had been expecting someone he would, of course, have let his visitor in.

"The door?" Shapiro said to one of the precinct men.

"No sign of anything. Not forced."

Shapiro walked over and looked at the fire tools beside the clean and empty fireplace. A poker, fire tongs and a hearth brush, all with brass tops and sturdy iron shafts. They looked clean enough. Shapiro did not touch them.

"Lab boys on the way," one of the precinct detectives said. "But the way it looks to me, he just fell and banged his head."

"The way it looks," Shapiro said, sadly. "Didn't seem to be the wobbly kind, but it could have been that way."

But it remained a coincidence and Nathan Shapiro does not like coincidences. His dislike, of course, does not prevent them from happening. Still —

"Elevator men?" Shapiro asked. "Any of them remember taking a stranger up to the twenty-second floor this afternoon?"

"Haven't got around to that, Lieutenant," the precinct man he spoke to said. "After all, we just got here when you showed up. Far as we've got, he just fell down and banged his head."

"Far as I've got too," Shapiro said. And, he thought, it was as far as he was going to get here. Talk to a doctor who had called the police because a man had fallen in the living room of his apartment. Shapiro rode down on a plummeting elevator, waited briefly for his stomach to rejoin him, and asked at the desk. Dr. Rolfe's office? That way. Shapiro went that way and found a door in a corridor with "E. J. Rolfe, M.D. By appointment" lettered on it. Shapiro pressed a button and heard a bell ring. He waited and pressed the button again, not hoping for anything to come of it. But a click came from it in the door's lock and a turned knob came of it and a tall, gray-haired man in a sober gray suit opened the door and said, "Yes?"

Shapiro said, "Dr. Rolfe?" and the tall man nodded his head.

"Police officer," Shapiro said and gave the rest of it. "About Mr. Agee."

He was told to come in and went into a waiting room with deep chairs in it and an air conditioner humming. Dr. Rolfe sat in one of the chairs and motioned toward another and said, "So, Lieutenant?"

"You called the police," Shapiro said. "About what apparently was a simple accident. Why, Doctor?"

"Les Agee's a friend of mine," Dr. Rolfe

said. He had a low, soothing voice. "As well as a patient. Mrs. Singleton gets stabbed to death. Her former husband falls and bashes his head. I thought the police might be interested."

"You thought perhaps he didn't fall? And hit his head on this andiron thing?"

"He certainly hit his head on something," Rolfe said. "Or got hit with something. The edge of the firedog. Or, say, a poker. The wound could have been made either way."

"It's bad," Shapiro said, not as a question.

Dr. Rolfe answered it as one. He said, "Damn bad, Lieutenant. Depressed fractures are always bad."

"He'll make it?"

Rolfe moved broad shoulders in a shrug.

"It's touch and go," he said. "He's got a good constitution. He'll need it."

"He's still unconscious?"

"Yes. And probably will be for a long time. If not for all time. Brain damage. We don't know how much. Pete Collins will have to go in to find out. Pete's a damn good surgeon. He'll need to be, I'm afraid."

"If Agee comes through, will he remember what happened?"

Rolfe shrugged again and opened his hands as his shoulders moved.

"Perhaps," he said. "Perhaps not. I'd be inclined to think that he won't. There'll be a gap, probably. Short gap. Long gap. Depends on what Pete finds and what he can do about what he finds. It'll be days, could be it'll be weeks, before we know." He paused and looked over Shapiro's head. "Could be," he said, "it'll be months."

Shapiro stood up and the doctor looked up at him.

"Les Agee," Rolfe said, "played tennis, Lieutenant. Pretty good at it. Had played for years."

Shapiro waited.

"Point is," Rolfe said, "tennis players learn to fall. I mean, to catch themselves. On their hands, usually. I wouldn't have expected Les to land on the back of his head. In fact, I wouldn't have expected him to fall at all. Ever see him, Lieutenant?"

"Yes," Shapiro said. "He looked fit. Moved well."

"Gave him a checkup two-three weeks ago," Rolfe said. "Very good shape then. Now, God knows, he'll need to be."

"You've no idea when we can talk to him?"

"I told you. Days. Weeks. Perhaps months. And perhaps never."

Nathan Shapiro went back by bus and subway to West Twentieth Street. They had not been able to get in touch with Detective Anthony Cook. No answer at his apartment. No answer at his girl's apartment. Not at Charles Restaurant, where he sometimes took this girl of his. In short, no Tony Cook.

But, a report from Cook on Shapiro's desk and in it one thing that might be salient. A thing about a retired general named Whitehall, who sat sometimes by his window across the street from the house Jennifer Singleton had died in. And who, on Sunday afternoon, had seen her on the sidewalk in front of her house talking with a man. Who had been turned in his wheel chair while she still was talking to a man who might have come with her in a taxi or might have been waiting for her outside her house. And who might, for all General Whitehall (Ret.) knew, have gone into her house with her. A small man in a dark suit, wearing a dark hat on a hot June afternoon.

Shapiro looked up the telephone number of Farmer, Rachel, who lived in Gay Street, and dialed the number and got no answer. He wrote his own report, after calling Brooklyn and telling Rose that, again, he might be late — and after being told, in a tone of resignation, that he was late already. Then, once again, he dialed an Algonquin number and a telephone rang in Gay Street. This time he was answered quickly by the girl and, a little less quickly, by Tony Cook, who apparently had been in another room. And Tony Cook would check it out. And when he had, sure he would come in.

Nathan Shapiro's stomach, which so often protested about so many things, usually in a rather nasty tone of voice, reminded him that he had not eaten for too many hours. Shapiro walked a few blocks to a restaurant, hoping that his stomach would be pleased with him. He had pot roast and mashed potatoes and ignored the carrots which came along. His stomach took the dimmest possible view of carrots.

Cook was not at the office when Shapiro got back to it. Shapiro sat at his desk and brooded. He wasn't getting anywhere. That much was evident, as it so often was. Probably, however agile he had appeared to be, Lester Agee had merely fallen and banged his head on iron. Got a foot stuck in an overdeep carpet — a carpet which had seemed to cling to Nathan Shapiro's own feet. Admit coincidence, whether you like it or not. And admit that, in all likelihood, precinct had been right in the first place — right about a tall, blond boy named Roy Baker.

A small man in a dark suit who had met Jennifer Singleton in front of her house, or who might have met her somewhere else and ridden to the house with her in a cab, probably had nothing to do with anything. A neighbor out for an afternoon stroll in warm sunshine meeting another neighbor and stopping briefly for a chat and then strolling on his way. It probably came to no more than that.

Shapiro ran through his mind the men he had talked to, the possibles he had told Bill Weigand and Dorian about, and measured them.

Lester Agee, presumably now on a hospital operating table — in all respects a big man. No angle of observation could foreshorten him to a small one. Joseph Gage. A tall man; as tall at least as Agee. And not, Shapiro thought, a man likely to be wearing a dark suit and a dark hat on a warm Sunday afternoon in June. Roy Baker. A tall boy, who would almost certainly not be wearing any hat at all and who had not, when captured, been wearing a dark suit. Kurt Morton, on the other hand — Morton was not tall; looked down on from a second floor window across a street he might well be thought of as a small man. And Morton probably bore a grudge.

The small man had been a strolling neighbor, his meeting with Jennifer Singleton during the last hour of her life a meeting by chance. A hundred to one that was the way it was. And if it came to making odds, a hundred to one precinct had been right about Roy Baker. A hundred to one, Nathan Shapiro thought, I'm merely mucking it up. As usual.

If Lester Agee had been hit on the head, which was not at all certain, it could be because Agee had seen more Sunday afternoon than he had admitted seeing. Got through the house to the garden, using a key he quite probably had, however he denied it, and found — found what? Found nobody at all, at an hour when Roy Baker was supposed to be there working? And — been seen by Baker from the window above, perhaps while Baker was going through Mrs. Singleton's bedroom looking for what he could steal? If Baker thought he had himself been seen he would have had reason — as violent men's reasons go — for silencing Lester Agee. Except, of course, that Agee had said nothing about going through the house to the garden or seeing anybody in the room above. No evident reason he shouldn't say he had if he had. But the kid wouldn't know that. Killers try not to take chances.

A fruitless spinning of theories, Shapiro decided of his thought process — a spinning of them and a tearing of them apart. And where the hell is Tony Cook?

Cook answered that by coming into Shapiro's small, hot office. He came in shaking his head.

"Kid was alone in the apartment when I got there," Cook said, and sat down across the desk from Nathan Shapiro. "Said he'd been alone there since he got home from school about four o'clock this afternoon. Said he'd been writing a story about a man who was unjustly suspected of murder. I said, 'How's about having a look at this story of yours, son?' and he said it hadn't worked out and he'd torn it up. He wanted to know why we wanted to know where he'd been and were we trying to pin something else on him, man."

"You tell him why, Tony?"

"Only that a man who knew Mrs. Singleton had had what was maybe an accident and maybe wasn't. It's been on the radio. All very no-comment. Interesting and regrettable co-incidence. With, sure, space between the lines for anybody who wants to read between them. And that Lester Agee, famed playwright, is in critical condition."

"Yes," Shapiro said. "He is, Tony. And his doctor doesn't think he's the kind to fall on the back of his head. And the lab's got a poker and a pair of fire tongs and hearth brush with thick shaft to play with. The boy can't prove he was in the apartment alone?"

"Doesn't try to."

"His father?"

"Working late. Store's open evenings and it's his turn to work evenings. I checked that out. True enough, and he's there now. Supposed to come on at five and work until midnight, only this afternoon he was maybe half an hour late."

"Left before the kid got home? And showed up late for work?"

"Way the kid tells it there was nobody in the apartment when he got home from school. Could be his old man was having a few beers somewhere and watching a ball game on TV. Could be, I suppose, he was uptown slugging Agee."

"Yes," Shapiro said. "The way it mostly is, Tony. Nothing to get hold of. This General Whitehall. Reliable old man?"

"Yes," Tony Cook said. "Lively old geezer, in spite of the wheel chair. Saw what he says he saw, I'm pretty certain."

"Which," Shapiro said, "wasn't enough. Your girl friend — Miss Farmer. Did she happen to know Mrs. Singleton? I suppose you asked her, since they both live — or did live — in the same general neighborhood."

"Rachel didn't know her," Tony said. "Knew her house. Used to walk past it thinking maybe Mrs. Singleton would come out and — anyway, Mrs. Singleton didn't come out. Rachel does know people who knew Mrs. Singleton, or say they did. All a lot younger than Mrs. Singleton was. Young playwrights and girls who want to be actresses and people like that. Nearest any of them came to knowing the lady was that one kid wrote a play and sent it to her because there was a part in it he thought might interest her."

"Did it?"

"From what he told Rachel it didn't. She sent it — the play — back to him, saying she was sorry. Saying nice things about the play, apparently, but that the character he had in mind for her should be played by an older woman. Which made him wonder if she'd really read the play because the character he'd had in mind for her was actually a lot younger than she was. And —"

"Yes, Tony," Nate Shapiro said. "Have a good evening?"

"Yes, Nate," Tony Cook said. "The evening was all right. Sorry I was out of touch. But —"

"It's all right," Shapiro said. "You were off duty. And — time we both were for the night. You're going home? Or — back to —"

"Home, Lieutenant. Just home. I walked one hell of a lot today and my feet hurt."

"It's a walking job," Nate said, and he and Cook walked together to the subway. The trains they took went in opposite directions.

A subway train is a bad place to think in; a thudding noisy place with discarded newspapers rustling on the floor. The rustling newspapers seemed a tickle in Nathan Shapiro's tired mind.

It was only when, in Brooklyn, he climbed gritty, cement steps from the track level that Shapiro realized it was not rustling newspapers which made a tickle in his mind.

XIV

It was pleasantly cool in the apartment, with the air conditioner on. Cleo stood on hind legs and pawed welcome against Nathan Shapiro's trousers, and he reached down and scratched her behind her most available ear. Rose put down a book and came across the living room to Nathan. She was wearing a white summer robe and her short black hair looked as if she had just washed it under the shower. She stood in front of her husband and looked up at him. She put her arms around him and, for a moment, held him close. Then she pushed him away a little and said, "You wear a most uncomfortable gun, Nathan. And you're tired, aren't you? And did you remember to have something to eat?"

"Yes," Nathan said. "I'm sorry about the gun, dear."

"Then take it off," Rose told him. "And sit down and I'll get us something cold to drink. Gin and tonic? I've been thinking of a gin and tonic."

"Iced tea," Nathan Shapiro said.

She shook her head at him. But she shrugged slim shoulders and went toward the kitchen. Shapiro sat down. He did not take his jacket off nor unbuckle his shoulder holster. He sat and left his mind free for the tickle in it. From the kitchen the teakettle whistled and then, after a minute or two, Rose came back, carrying a tray with ice tinkling in two tall glasses. She put the tray down on a table and, still standing, looked down at Nathan.

"You're home," she said. "You can take your coat off at home. And your gun off at home. Unless — *Nathan.* Are you going to —"

"Perhaps I'll have to," Nathan said. "After a glass of tea."

"You're tired," she said. She brought him tea and they sat side by side on a sofa which faced an empty fireplace. "It's about Mrs. Singleton, isn't it? And — it wasn't as simple as they thought, was it? They've let Roy go, haven't they? It was on the radio."

"Reduced his bail," Nathan said, and sipped from his glass. The coldness of the glass pleased his hand. He hoped his stomach would approve the tea. It had no immediate comment. "The mother of his girl friend put up the bond money. So he was free — could have been free — to try to kill a man named Agee."

She repeated the name. She said, "The playwright? Why would he? Has he been arrested again?"

Nathan shook his head slowly.

"Rose," he said, "this teacher of his. The man who thinks the kid's got talent."

"Clarke Pierson?"

"Yes. Can you tell me anything about him?"

"He's a qualified man. Doctorate from Columbia. He's taught at the school for several years. He's well thought of as a teacher. No, Nathan, I don't really know him. He seems — oh, a little wispy. But I'm only beginning to know the teachers at Clayton."

"He told me he'd written a play several years ago," Shapiro said. "That it was put on and flopped. That he hadn't written one since. You knew about that, Rose?"

"Oh," she said, "*about* him. Yes. Things get around. He was a writer before he became a teacher. Magazine stories, I think. Or, anyway, stories intended for magazines. And this play of his that flopped — yes, I've heard about that."

"Wanted to be a writer," Shapiro said, as much to himself as to his wife. "Turned out to be teaching kids how to write."

"I know," Rose said. "Those who can, do; those who can't, teach. It's not especially true, dear."

"Of Pierson?"

She turned her glass between her fingers

slowly and looked at the empty fireplace.

"Perhaps," she said. "Oh, perhaps, Nathan. Why are you interested in poor little Dr. Pierson? He is a doctor, you know. Of philosophy. Because he once wrote a play that failed?"

"I heard something today," Shapiro said. "Cook did, rather. From this Rachel of his."

"Who," Rose said, "Is quite a girl. What did Tony Cook hear?"

"That sometimes playwrights send copies of their plays to actors. Plays they think have parts in for the actors they send them to. Do you know if that happens?"

"Oh, yes," Rose Shapiro said. "I've heard it happens. And?"

"I don't know the 'and,' " Shapiro said. "Probably something I'm just fumbling with, as usual."

"Sometimes," Rose said, "you make me mad, my darling. Sometimes you make me very mad indeed. That 'as usual' business. Because it isn't that at all. As I keep telling you over and over. You do not fumble. Repeat that after me."

He turned to face her and smiled the smile which so greatly, if for the most part so briefly, changed his sad face.

"Teacher," Nathan said, "I do not fumble. I do not fumble. And I am quite good with a gun, too. Do you know anything more about

260

Clarke Pierson? How old he is? Whether he's married."

"In his early forties," Rose said. "It'll be in the records if it matters. Yes, he's married. And he and his wife have a child, I think. Perhaps they have two children."

"Does he make much?"

"None of us makes much, Nathan. He — enough to live on. That'll be in the records too, of course."

"And where he lives?"

Rose did not know. She thought somewhere in the Village. Within walking distance of the school. She did not know what made her think that. O — she did know, of course.

"I was a little late a week or so ago," she said. "Was walking to the subway station. And saw him. He was walking south on Seventh Avenue and carrying what looked like a bag of groceries. As if, I thought, he was carrying it home. I remember thinking the bag looked too heavy for him and hoping that he didn't have to carry it too far. He doesn't look strong, does he?"

"Not especially," Nathan said. "As you said, a little wispy. Of course, they fool you sometimes. Sometimes the word is wiry, not wispy. He was at the school today?"

So far as Rose Shapiro knew, Clarke Pierson had taken his classes that day at Clayton High

School. His day would have ended at four in the afternoon — could have ended then. He might, of course, have stayed on in his classroom and read papers his pupils had written.

"I wonder," Shapiro said, "whether Pierson is in the telephone book."

He went to another room where he keeps telephone directories of New York's five boroughs. One can never tell in what borough information waits to be uncovered.

Clarke Pierson lived on Charlton Street. Shapiro noted the number in his mind and went back to what was left of his iced tea, and to Rose. Rose was almost certain that Charlton Street was in the Village. She said, *"Nathan!"*

"I'm afraid so," Nathan Shapiro said. "Couple of questions I'd like to ask Mr. Pierson. Stupid questions, probably."

Rose Shapiro said, "Damn." Nathan Shapiro used the telephone. Tony Cook, who had taken to spending a good deal of his off-duty time in Greenwich Village, probably would know where Charlton Street was.

The apartment house in Charlton Street was six stories tall and looked as if it were tired of holding itself up. The small lobby was dingy and dimly lighted. Cook flicked his cigarette lighter on and moved it up and down in front of the slots in which tenants had listed their names until he found the name they wanted. Clarke Pierson lived in Apartment 6A. There was an old and reluctant elevator which creaked a little as it lifted them toward the sixth floor. The sixth floor corridor was even more dimly lighted than the lobby. They found a door with "6A" lettered on it, and Cook pushed a button beside it. There was an unexpectedly loud clatter from inside. After a few moments there were footfalls inside, and the door opened to the extent of a safety chain.

"Wispy" was, Shapiro thought, more than ever the word for the man who partly opened the door. "Wispy" was the word for the pale hair he smoothed down as he looked out at, and up at, the two tall men. He wore a white shirt, open at the neck, and dark trousers.

"Police lieutenant," Shapiro said, and gave his name, and Pierson said, "Oh. You again. I told you all I know about the boy. And my wife's asleep."

"We won't be long," Shapiro said. "And we'll try to keep our voices down, Mr. Pierson. Just one or two more points you can maybe help us with."

"About the boy?"

"I'm afraid so," Shapiro told the small man, who kept on smoothing his hair, although it no longer needed smoothing. "Something else has come up that may involve the boy."

"I told you all I know about him," Pierson said. "He's a good student. He has a good mind. As kids go, he writes well."

"More or less about that," Shapiro said. "Kind of things he writes. Might, we thought, show the kind of kid he is. This is Detective Cook, by the way. Working with me on Mrs. Singleton's murder." He paused for a moment, as if he hesitated about going on. When he said, "And the attack on Mr. Agee. Which may turn out to be another homicide. We don't know yet."

"Agee?" Pierson said. "Somebody's attacked Agee?" he sounded incredulous. He sounded like a man who had not, that evening, listened to radio news.

"Yes," Shapiro said. "Anyhow, it looks that way now. Looked at first like an accident, but now it looks as if he got hit with a poker. And, of course, as if the killing of Mrs. Singleton and this attack on Agee might be related."

"I don't see —" Pierson said, and shrugged his narrow shoulders. "But, all right. Come on in."

He unlocked the chain and opened the door. They followed him into a small room. Somebody had been cooking onions in the apartment. Pierson had left a pipe smoldering when he went to the door. He drew on it and shook his head and relighted it. He sat in a chair by the table on which the pipe had been resting in an ashtray. Then he got up and went to a door which opened off the small room and closed the door.

"Want her to sleep if she can," he said. "She's not well. Not at all well. Needs what rest she can get. What about the things Roy Baker writes, Lieutenant? Strange line of inquiry, it seems to me. Was he the one hit Les Agee with a poker?"

"We don't know," Shapiro said. "We follow all lines of inquiry, Mr. Pierson. Never can tell what we may turn up. And you know this boy, maybe, as well as anybody. You're an educated man and, I'd guess, a perceptive one. It's like consulting an expert, in a way. Not a field Cook here and I know much about."

"Field?"

"Writing field," Shapiro said. "This kid's probably written a good many things for this class you teach. Stories? That sort of thing?"

"Stories," Pierson said. "Essays. Young Baker's written fiction, mostly."

"What kind?"

"Well," Pierson said, "pretty gloomy stuff, for the most part. But most of what the kids write is gloomy nowadays. They — oh, say they take a dim view of the world. It's a tense generation, Lieutenant. In some respects a desperate one. Understandably, it seems to me."

"These stories young Baker wrote," Shapiro said. "Violent stories? Make you feel — oh, that there's violence in the boy. Comes out in what he writes?"

"Yes. But that doesn't mean that he'd do violent things. Sometimes, when they're writers, or are wanting to be writers, writing acts as a release, you know. A — one might call it a transference. A sublimation, in a sense. See what I mean?"

Shapiro said he guessed so. He said it wasn't anything he knew much about. He spoke sadly, in a low voice, as of one who mourned his own ignorance.

"One story young Baker wrote," Pierson said, "was about a mugging. From the point of view of one of the kids who had mugged an old man. A vivid piece, for a kid. Real and vivid. But that doesn't mean that Roy had ever mugged anybody. Merely that he could imagine it."

"Sure," Shapiro said. "But it might show there was potential violence in the boy, wouldn't you say? That his imagination ran to violent things?"

"Probably there's violence in all of us," Pierson said. "Potential violence. Writers express it in words. In make believe. But I'm a school teacher, lieutenant. Not a psychiatrist. I can't tell you whether Roy is the kind to hit a man on the back of the head with a poker. Wouldn't be evidence if I tried to guess. You've got real evidence that he attacked Agee?"

"Looking for it," Shapiro said. "Nothing, yet, actually, to pin it on him. Mrs. Singleton is killed and maybe the kid kills her. Mr. Agee knew her. Had been married to her and written a lot of plays for her. And somebody tries to kill Agee."

"I thought young Baker was being held as a material witness."

"Out on bail," Shapiro said. "Released several hours before Agee was attacked this afternoon. And Agee was down at Mrs. Singleton's house Sunday. Was going to take her to dinner, apparently. Thing is, he may have seen something."

"Something that would incriminate the boy?"

Shapiro said it could have been that way. Or, of course, that the boy thought Agee had; perhaps was just afraid he had.

"Murderers get frightened," Shapiro said. "Get — oh, to imagining they've made mistakes. Sometimes ones they haven't really made. But they can't take chances. Have to

267

try to clean everything up. Like whoever used a poker to hit Agee with tried to clean the poker up. Wipe it with something. Maybe with his own handkerchief. Wiped prints off and tried to wipe blood and hair off. And fragments of skin."

"He failed?"

"Far as identifiable prints go, no. But the lab boys found blood and several hairs on the shaft of the poker. Hard to get a thing like a poker clean when it's been used the way this one was."

Tony Cook looked intently at Shapiro, as if he were about to say something. He didn't say anything.

"Violence in the boy," Shapiro said and nodded his head. "Came out in what he wrote. Not proof of anything, as you say, Mr. Pierson. Just — call it maybe a hint of something."

"Not even that, I'd think," Pierson said. "It's a violent world, Lieutenant. A harsh world. Not a world for drawing-room comedies like the things Agee's still writing. A world filled with angry young men."

"Oh," Shapiro said. "It always has been. Violence takes different forms at different times. Speaking of plays, Mr. Pierson. Roy ever write a play for your class?"

"No."

"The kids are free to write plays if they

want to? As a playwright yourself, I'd think you might have encouraged them to."

"Schoolteacher," Pierson said. "Schoolteacher who once thought he could write plays. I told you that, Lieutenant. One of the boys in this creative writing class did a play a few weeks ago. Frivolous bit of nothing. Like the plays Agee's been writing all his life. Like, come down to it, this thing of his poor Jennifer was in."

"I didn't see it," Shapiro said. "You did, didn't you Tony?"

"Yes," Tony said. "Seemed all right to me. You saw the play, Mr. Pierson?"

"Last week," Pierson said. "Passé bit of nothing. Old hat. And, the thing is, it needn't have been. The general situation — he could have made a play out of it. He turned it into chatter. Wisecracks he thought were epigrams. Without Jenny and that laugh of hers it couldn't have lasted a week. He missed the whole point of it. Didn't you really feel that, Mr. Cook?"

"I don't know," Tony Cook said. "Seemed pretty funny to me. Most of the time, anyway."

Pierson leaned forward in his chair. He looked a little as if he were about to jump out of it. And when he spoke his voice went up.

"That's just it," he said. "That's precisely

what's the matter with it. Same thing as is the matter with most of what Agee writes. Takes a situation which isn't a comedy situation and twists it out of shape to make it comedy. Here's this woman, successful in her own world, traps herself in another. In a world where she's lost. Tries to adjust to the life and to the man — the people — who make it. And the effort nibbles away at her — at what she really is, until there's nothing left of her. Not tragedy in the big sense. Just — just slow disintegration. Not, God knows, a tinkling little joke, like what Agee turned it into."

He leaned back suddenly in his chair and knocked his pipe clean and slowly filled it again. His hands, Shapiro thought, were a little shaky.

"Sorry," Pierson said when he had stuffed his pipe. He lighted it. "Something of a tirade, that. Just that I hate to see good ideas loused up the way this one was. A tirade, way off the subject."

"Perhaps it was Mrs. Singleton's doing," Shapiro said. "What you call the twisting of *Always Good-bye*, that is. Seems the idea was partly hers. Agee says so, anyway. And he was sharing his royalties with her because it was. You know about the theater, Mr. Pierson. Isn't that a little unusual?"

Pierson said, "What?" like a man who had not been listening. Then he said, "I don't know, Lieutenant. I never had any royalties to share. You say she suggested the idea?"

"Agee says so. In some detail, I gather. Says she'd had ideas for plays before. For her to star in. And that none of the other ideas was worth much. He seemed surprised that this one was. Could be she got the idea from somebody else. Think that's possible, Mr. Pierson?"

"How the hell would I know?" Pierson said. "And what's it got to do with what you're after, anyway?"

"Probably nothing," Nathan Shapiro said. "Like this woman in the play — I'm trying to adjust to a life I don't know anything about. Just groping around. Come on a man like yourself, who's knowledgeable about such things, and I muddle along trying to get things straight. Bad habit of mine."

"A waste of time, anyway," Pierson said. "This bit of froth of Agee's can't, so far as I see, have anything to do with who killed Jenny Singleton. And, if it was that way, hit Agee on the back of the head. I'd think you'd look for something more — tangible."

"Oh," Shapiro said. "We do that too, Mr. Pierson. Just now we're looking for a rather small man who wore a dark suit and a dark hat on a hot Sunday afternoon. And who either went to Mrs. Singleton's house with her an hour or so before she was killed or had been waiting for her to come. Or, of course, merely met her by chance in front of the house."

"Somebody see a man like that?"

"Yes, Mr. Pierson. Somebody did. Very clearly. Looking down from a window across the street. Pretty sure he can identify him if he sees him again, General Whitehall is."

Cook looked again at Nathan Shapiro. Again, Cook didn't say anything.

"A break for us, maybe that is," Shapiro said. "We have to count on breaks a good deal, Mr. Pierson. Old men look out windows and see things nobody can count on their seeing. It'll help, maybe."

"You say yourself it may have been just acquaintances meeting by accident," Pierson said. He had his pipe going well. The smoke was acrid. Probably, Nathan Shapiro thought, the little man can't afford very good tobacco.

"That's right," Shapiro said. "Probably get us nowhere even if we find the man. We're asking around the neighborhood, all the same. Ask all sorts of questions which don't get us anywhere. Turn up little odds and ends which don't add to anything. For example — tell him what this friend of yours told you last

272

night, Tony. About playwrights sometimes sending —"

"I don't —" Cook said and then, quickly, nodded his head and said, "Oh. That. Sending playscripts to actors. That what you mean, Lieutenant?"

"Yes," Shapiro said. "One of the odds and ends. Bits of information — irrelevant information, probably — we pick up as we go along."

"Seems," Cook said, "people who write plays sometimes send copies of them to actors and actresses they think might be interested in working in them. In the plays, I mean. Who might, the playwright hopes, take the plays to producers and say, 'This is one I want to act in,' or something like that. Man this friend of mine knows did send a script to Mrs. Singleton, he says. And that she read it, but didn't see anything in it for her."

"You know the theater, Mr. Pierson," Shapiro said. "That sort of thing happen very often, do you know?"

"I've heard it happens," Pierson said. "People do send plays to stars, I guess."

"Seems a bit risky to me," Shapiro said. "Of course, in my job, you can get to take a dim view of people."

Pierson drew on his pipe, which gurgled, and exhaled smoke. He said he didn't get what

Shapiro was driving at.

"Not at anything, probably," Shapiro said. "Play scripts. I suppose they're copyrighted?"

"Not usually," Pierson said. "You mean somebody — some actor, say — might read a play and have it copied or something?"

"I just wondered," Shapiro said. "Whole business is new to me. Or — just steal the basic idea, perhaps. What you call the situation. Like the situation in this play of Agee's you say he twisted out of shape. What I mean about its being risky, Mr. Pierson."

"Can't say I ever heard of anything like that happening," Pierson said.

"Probably I've just got a suspicious mind," Shapiro said. "I'm supposed to have, of course. Well — we've taken up a lot of your time, Mr. Pierson. Sorry about your wife. She's in a pretty bad way?"

"Pretty bad," Pierson said. "If I could send her to a big clinic. Like Mayo's. Sort of thing costs a lot of money. Not the kind of money a schoolteacher has."

"My wife," Shapiro said, "tells me you've got a couple of children, Mr. Pierson. They here in the apartment?"

"No," Pierson said. "Jane's not up to — to taking care of them just now. They're with her mother."

Shapiro said, "Well," again. This time he

stood up. He looked down at Clarke Pierson, who started to get up out of his own chair.

"One thing I'm sort of puzzled about," Shapiro said. "Couple of times you've spoken about Agee's being hit on the back of the head. He was. But — *how did you know it, Mr. Pierson?*"

"Heard it on the radio," Pierson said. He put his pipe down in the ashtray.

"No," Shapiro said. "I don't think so. Because we haven't given out any details like that, Mr. Pierson. Just that Mr. Agee fell in his apartment and badly hurt himself. That's all that's been on the radio, Mr. Pierson."

"I suppose I just guessed it then," Pierson said. "Most likely place to hit a man if you're going to use a poker."

"Yes," Shapiro said. "Say a man is sitting in a chair and you're behind him with a poker. The chair has a low back, maybe, and his head comes up above it. Pretty vulnerable position the man is in, isn't it?"

Pierson looked up at Shapiro. He looked up with widening eyes.

"Did you send a play to Mrs. Singleton, Mr. Pierson? For her to read because you thought she could act the leading role? Because — wait a minute. The situation, as you tell it, could be a little like her own life, couldn't it? When she left the stage and married Singleton and tried to adjust to living the kind of life rich people do on Long Island estates? Or did then. You sent her a play, Mr. Pierson?"

"No," Pierson said. "I didn't send her a play."

"Settles that," Shapiro said. "You first saw her in this play of Agee's last week. This play you say he twisted out of the shape it should have been in. You hadn't seen it before."

"No."

"I think," Shapiro said, "that it was quite a shock when you did see it, Mr. Pierson. What was its title when you sent it to her to read? Not, I suppose, *Always Good-bye*. Something more —"

"*The Shallow* —" Pierson said, and heard his own voice and seemed to panic as Shapiro had thought he might.

Pierson came up out of the chair, his right hand in his trousers pocket.

The hand came out with something in it, and a blade leaped out of the handle of a switchblade knife.

Shapiro's own right hand shot under his jacket for his gun, but he didn't need it. Tony Cook was quicker than either of them, and he didn't reach for his gun. He slashed his hand down, holding it edgewise, on the small man's wrist, and the knife flew out of the

276

smaller hand. He grabbed Pierson and held him in hard hands.

Shapiro snapped the blade back into the knife, not bothering about fingerprints because they wouldn't come into it. But he was careful not to touch the blade.

It is hard to clean a knife of blood — to clean it so a police laboratory cannot find traces even after many hours, and from the traces identify a type. It is even harder to be sure you have got a knife clean than it is to be sure about a poker.

XV

Anthony Cook was tired. He had been up most of the night before and slept a few hours and gone on duty again, working on odds and ends. But, late in the afternoon as he walked down Sixth Avenue from Fourteenth Street, he did not walk like a tired man. He walked like a man who was going somewhere and wanted to get where he was going.

He saw the kids at Ninth Street. They were on the east side of Sixth and waiting for the light to change so they could cross it. They were nice-looking kids. Roy Baker was a lot taller than the girl and had a long arm around her waist, and she had her arm as far around the big boy as it would go. When he got down to Eighth Street and was waiting for a light himself, Tony Cook looked back. The kids were walking, still holding on to each other, down toward Eighth. Ellen was still looking up at Roy and they didn't seem to be paying much attention to where they were going. But people veered around them. People who walk

278

Village streets, if they are considerate people, get used to giving right of way to engrossed young couples.

Maybe she'll persuade him to get his hair cut, Tony Cook thought, and himself veered away. He veered off Sixth Avenue toward Gay Street. The nearer he got to Gay Street the nearer he came to forgetting that he was tired.

She had on a white dress, this time. As nearly as Tony could remember it was the same white dress she had worn when he had first seen her in a dress. She held the apartment door open and for a moment looked at him from eyes nearly level with his own.

"You look tired, mister," Rachel Farmer said. "I've got everything ready, and you just sit down."

He did as he was told, and it was she who went to the kitchen and got her sherry and the chilled glass for it out of the refrigerator. It was she who put ice into his glass and poured bourbon on it and said, "You can take your gun off now. It shows." He took his gun off. It was pleasant to do as he was told.

"The poor little man talked," Rachel said. "At least the *Times* says he did. Or that you and Lieutenant Shapiro allege he did."

"The lieutenant," Tony said. "And Captain Weigand. And Assistant District Attorney Bernard Simmons. They allege. I just sit in.

He sure as hell talked. Nobody could stop his talking. Not that anybody tried very hard. Oh, he was told he didn't have to talk. And advised that he should have a lawyer present if he did want to talk. And he just went on talking and it went on tape. Until damn near four o'clock this morning it went on tape."

He sighed, remembering again that he was tired. He was told to drink his drink and did as he was told. He was told he didn't look comfortable there and to come over here, and he went and sat on the sofa beside the girl who was almost as tall as he was.

"We don't have to go anywhere," Rachel said. "I've got things we can eat when we want to eat. What did you mean on the telephone when you said I'd helped?"

"Told me something I hadn't known," Tony said. "Didn't mean anything to me, but I happened to pass it on to the lieutenant and he got a hunch. And tried it out on Pierson and Pierson panicked. I hadn't expected him to, but I guess Nate had. Says he was as surprised as I was because he never knows what people are like, but that's something he always says. He did press a little, the lieutenant did. Surprised me once or twice. Told Pierson the lab boys had found blood and hair on the poker. They hadn't yet. Or, anyway, hadn't sent through a report on it. And he told Pierson that General Whitehall would be able to identify the man Mrs. Singleton was talking to, which Whitehall can't do. Could have been it was that, as much as anything, made Pierson panic. That and the realization he'd slipped up himself by knowing more about where Agee was hit than he could have known. And —"

"I wish," Rachel said, "you'd begin at the beginning. Or, for that matter, begin anywhere. What did I tell you that helped?"

"That playwrights sometimes send scripts to actors," Tony said. "I hadn't known that. Shapiro hadn't known that. Gave him his hunch about Pierson."

"Pierson did that? Sent a script to — oh, to Jennifer Singleton? If that was in the *Times* it was in the jump and mostly I don't jump."

Pierson had said he had; he had said it over and over once he had begun to talk uncontrollably. To explain himself over and over as if being understood was more important than admitting to murder. That he had sent the script of a play called *The Shallow Pool* to Jennifer Singleton, because it was, to a degree, about her and that she and Lester Agee had stolen it — had turned it into a worthless charade called *Always Good-bye*.

"He says he went to Mrs. Singleton to get what was due him," Cook told the girl beside him. "Didn't have any idea of killing her. Just

281

happened to have the switchblade — which he says he took away from one of the boys at the school — in his pocket. That he hadn't meant to use it, though now he guesses he must have."

"He doesn't sound very sane," Rachel said.

"In Bellevue under observation now," Tony told her. "They're trying to find out. And his wife's at St. Vincent's. She's got this blood cancer — leukemia — and's going to die of it. There's nothing much anybody can do about it. Which Pierson couldn't get himself to admit. He kept thinking that if he could only get the money he thought he had coming to him he could do something for her."

"I'm sorry for him," Rachel said. "I hope they find out at the hospital he's too nuts to be responsible."

"He killed a woman," Cook said. "Tried to kill a man."

"Because they'd stolen from him," Rachel said. "They had?"

It was not as clear as that, Tony Cook told her. Pierson had written a play called *The Shallow Pool*. They had found a carbon of the manuscript in his apartment. It was being checked with the script of *Always Good-bye*. That was being done at the District Attorney's office, and the man on it was still cagey. But he had found "certain similarities," for what that was worth. They had only Pierson's own word for it that he had sent the script to Mrs. Singleton — and that she had kept it almost three months and then sent it back, saying it wasn't for her.

"Agee did tell the lieutenant that the idea for *Always Good-bye* was partly Mrs. Singleton's," Cook said. "It could be — Nate thinks it could be — that she wasn't really conscious where her idea came from and that it may have come from Pierson's play without her actually knowing it. And that Agee himself may not have known anything about Pierson's play."

Agee would be asked about that when, and if, he could be asked about anything. "They think now he'll make it. He's still in a coma, and nobody knows what he'll remember when he comes out of it."

Pierson had not thought the use of the situation from his play was subconscious on Jennifer Singleton's part. He had thought it theft. He had telephoned her on Friday, the day after he had first seen *Always Good-bye*. He had asked if he could see her Sunday afternoon, said he wanted to ask her something about the play she was in. She had said he might come Sunday; that she expected to be home around four. She had been later than that and Pierson, after ringing the bell and getting no answer, had waited for her in front of the house.

"Remember," Cook told the girl, "this is what Pierson tells us is the way it was."

"I'll remember," Rachel said, and her lips crinkled. "You're not in court testifying, Tony. You're with a girl friend. Finish your drink, mister."

Tony raised his glass and sipped from it and looked over it at the girl. She raised her own glass. She had fine, long hands, Tony thought. They distracted him.

"He went in with her," Rachel said. "And he accused her of stealing his play. And what? Wanted to be paid for it?"

It had come to that, Tony Cook supposed. It had not, apparently, been as simple as that. "It was what they'd done to it," Pierson had said, and said many times during the long hours during which, with few questions necessary or asked, he had talked on and on. "That was the main thing. They'd made it into trash. She and Agee."

But he had asked for money. That he did not deny.

Jennifer Singleton had at first denied she knew what he was talking about; had said that she didn't remember anything about a play he had sent her. Oh, he had sent her one. She could not remember whether she actually had read it. Certainly she had not stolen it, or from it.

"She called me a crazy little man," Clarke Pierson told the listening policeman and the man from the District Attorney's office. His voice went up to shrillness as he said that. "And she laughed at me. *Laughed* at me!"

He had said he wanted money — half, anyway, of what she and Agee had made out of the play. "I ought to have had it all," Pierson told his listeners. "I was being fair, wasn't I? Wasn't I being fair?"

Nobody answered that.

He had told Jennifer Singleton that his wife was sick and that he needed money to have her taken care of. Jennifer had told him that that was an old, old story. But she had said she would give him something and that he could call it charity. She had said, five hundred dollars if he would promise not to tell this crazy story of his around. Not that anybody would believe it — anybody who counted. She had said it was a matter of the nuisance value and looked at him and laughed again at him and said, "You *are* a nuisance, little man. A piddling little nuisance. I'd thought you might be, so after you called me up I wrote Les about you."

"If she did say that," Rachel said, "it sounds as if she knew what he was going to charge her with. Her and Agee. Doesn't it? If she wrote Mr. Agee before she'd seen Pierson?"

"It's only the way he says it was," Cook said. "Maybe he's lying. Maybe — oh, I don't know. Maybe he just thinks it was that way. He got pretty hysterical toward the end. Most of the time, actually, he was — call it wild. Panic wild."

Pierson had told Jennifer Singleton that ten times five hundred wouldn't be half enough. "I told her I needed thousands, not hundreds," he told those who listened to him in a small, hot and smoky room in the West Twentieth Street precinct house. He had told her he had it coming to him. She had laughed again. She had said, "Sue us, little man. Sue Les and me. Let everybody in on the laugh, little man."

But she had got up then and gone from the upstairs living room, to which she had taken him, toward her bedroom. She had told him she was going to get her checkbook and give him his "tip."

"She called it a tip," Pierson had said. "A tip!"

He had followed her into the bedroom and it must — he thought it must — have been then he got his knife out. "I didn't mean to hurt her. I'm sure I didn't mean to hurt her. Just — just to scare that laughing out of her."

He had found her in the bedroom, not taking

a checkbook out of a dressing table drawer but lifting the telephone by her bed. She had laughed again before she saw the knife and had said, "You're out the five hundred, little man. I'm calling the police and —"

Then she had seen the knife in his hand and seen the blade leap out of it. She had run, but there was not room to run in. She had got around the big bed and he had grabbed her from behind and —

"It's all mixed up now," he had told them. "The way things are in a nightmare. I guess I reached around and stuck the knife into her. I was holding her with an arm around her neck. I think that was the way it was. And — and she just sort of slipped out of my arm. It seems as if that was the way it was."

"Do you," Rachel said, "you and the others, think it was really that way? That he really — oh, didn't know what he was doing? What? Temporary insanity? Is that what they call it?"

"He brought a knife with him," Tony said. "He killed her with the knife. Lawyers and psychiatrists can argue about the rest of it."

"And Agee? He went to Agee for money, too? But without the knife?"

"If he had the knife he didn't use it," Cook said. "To have another try at getting money, yes, he says so. But — if Mrs. Singleton had written Agee saying that a little man named

Pierson was bothering her, and then turned up dead, Agee would sure as hell have put the two things together."

Pierson had used a different approach in getting an appointment with Lester Agee. He had said he wanted to ask a favor. He said that Agee had been sympathetic once and that he hadn't forgotten it and wondered if he could show Agee another play. One he had just finished. And Agee had told him to come along and fixed a time and, when Pierson went along, had let him in. When he was in, Pierson had made the same demands he had made on Jennifer Singleton — the same demands and the same accusations.

"He thought it was funny," Pierson told those who let him talk in the small, hot precinct room, while all he said went on tape. "Funny, the lousy, wisecracking clown. He laughed the way she'd laughed. He said, 'Get out of here, small-timer.' "

Pierson said that Agee had started for him, then, as if he planned to throw him out, and that it was then he had grabbed the poker. After he had used it he had wiped it off with his handkerchief and pulled the big, unconscious man so that his broken head was against the edge of the firedog. That was the way he remembered it had been — remembered as another nightmare.

Rachel finished her sherry and sat for a moment looking at the small empty glass. She shook her head.

"Mrs. Singleton hadn't written Mr. Agee, then," she said, to the small glass. "Because if she had Agee wouldn't have let poor little Mr. Pierson come to see him."

"Yes," Cook said, and finished what was in his own glass. "She'd written him. But he hadn't opened the letter. We found it today on his desk, with half a dozen other letters he hadn't opened. In it she said — I don't remember, exactly — said that a little twerp named Pierson was apparently trying to make a nuisance of himself."

"Did Mr. Agee know she had got the idea for the play from Pierson's play?"

"*If* she did," Cook said. "About Agee, we haven't the faintest idea. Maybe he knew and maybe he didn't know. We'll ask him, if we can ever ask him anything."

He spoke slowly, in a tired voice.

"I'll make us drinks," Rachel Farmer said. "And then I'll open something for us to eat."

Tony Cook held his glass out to her, and up to her.

"I ought to do it," Tony said. "After all, I'm taller than you are."